# DEVIL'S GOLD

# DEVIL'S GOLD

## Chet Cunningham

Chivers Press   •   G.K. Hall & Co.
Bath, Avon, England      Thorndike, Maine USA

This Large Print edition is published by Chivers Press, England, and by
G.K. Hall & Co., USA.

Published in 1996 in the U.K. by arrangement with the author.

Published in 1995 in the U.S. by arrangement with Chet Cunningham.

U.K. Hardcover  ISBN  0–7451–2886–6  (Chivers Large Print)
U.S. Softcover    ISBN  0–7838–1238–8  (Nightingale Collection
                                                        Edition)

The text of this Large Print edition is unabridged.
Other aspects of the book may vary from the original edition.

Set in 16 pt. New Times Roman.

Printed in Great Britain on acid-free paper.

**British Library Cataloguing in Publication Data available**

**Library of Congress Cataloging-in-Publication Data**

Cunningham, Chet.
   Devil's gold : Jim Steel / Chet Cunningham.
      p.   cm.
   ISBN  0–7838–1238–8  (lg. print : lsc)
   1. Large type books.   I. Title.
[PS3553.U468D48   1995]
813'.54—dc20                                                          95–11098

## CHAPTER ONE

# DEVIL'S GULCH CAMP JUSTICE

Jim Steel rode steadily along the winding trail, following a stream that meandered higher and higher into the mountains. He had been in the saddle since early morning with a sad-faced mule called Grouchy trailing on a lead rope behind his big buckskin, Hamlet. No stage coach traveled into Devil's Gulch, and no supply wagon would be going in until one came out for more food, shovels, and pans. The trail was little more than a faint scratch through the wilderness, and not even that had been here two months ago.

The rider sat the horse with the ease of long experience, yet his nonchalance was undergirded with trigger quick responses, and eyes that took in everything as far ahead on the trail as he could see. He was not a man often surprised.

Steel was tall, with the sun- and wind-marked face of an outdoorsman, but his hands were not calloused and rope-burned to peg him as a cowhand. His face was long and thin like the rest of him, more handsome than plain, but the first quality in it a stranger noticed was strength, supported with a raw toughness and confidence.

It was a forty-mile ride from Durango to Devil's Gulch, and Jim wasn't pushing. He used the time to figure out exactly how he should play his hand once he came into the rough and bloody mining camp. He'd seen dozens of them before and he knew that this one would be much the same: a wilderness, a thin little stream, dampness and cold everywhere, the stink of hundreds of men crammed together along the water or in a canyon, a scattering of tents and never enough food, heat or whiskey. There would be tempers fraying and breaking continually and no women or law and order to keep the men in line.

He let the big buckskin stop and drop his head to tongue off a mouth of grass.

It was 1867 and the whole West was growing, booming. The great surge of people over the trails into the territories continued. Civilization was reaching out to touch more and more of the frontier. The people back East were laughing about Secretary of State Seward's purchase of Alaska from Russia for seven million dollars. They called it Seward's Folly. Jim read that in London John Stuart Mill's bill to permit English women to vote was rejected by Parliament. In June of 1867 Mexico executed Emperor Maximilian, and the same year the Dominion of Canada was established in the far north.

Jim thought about these things and then

2

about Denver where he had been catching up on his newspaper reading and a few good meals when he noticed an item in the Denver *Rocky Mountain News*. It was a small death story item on page ten about Ted McIntosh.

*Friends of Theodore McIntosh, late of this city, learned here this week that he died recently in the Devil's Gulch mining camp north of Durango. Witnesses said McIntosh evidently was working on a sluice box in the river when the heavy plank trough gave way, pinning him underwater. When found the next morning he had expired.*

Jim had studied the item for many minutes before he tore it from the paper. Ted McIntosh was a hard rock miner, not a free gold man. There was little chance that he would be panning for gold or working a sluice. Besides, none of the small boxes in those little rivers around Durango were heavy enough to hold Ted McIntosh underwater—not unless somebody was there helping.

Ted usually could take care of himself. Only this time someone had killed him. Jim was positive of that. Why?

Jim thought it through, discarding the obvious reasons. Ted was not a brawler, not a fighter, wouldn't jump some gold panner's stretch of cold water. But a problem over a big strike might do it. That Jim would fight for.

3

Ted had worked hard rock mines with Jim three different times, once as partners they had taken over $100,000 worth of high grade gold ore from the ground, and parted two years later with a profit of $25,000 each.

Jim had packed a valise, withdrawn five hundred dollars in gold from his account at Denver National and caught the stage for Durango with his favorite mount trotting along behind on a lead.

Now, he sat hip shot, his right foot cocked on the saddle as he scanned the country with clear blue eyes, always alert, taking in everything as if he were a lead scout on an army patrol. Jim Steel stood an inch under six feet when the average man's height was five-feet-five. He had thick black hair that crowded down on his forehead and hid both ears. Jim wore a heavy black mustache and long sideburns to help protect his face. His skin had the look of a man who spent more nights under the stars than under a comforter. Jim was hard and lean, as supple and lithe as a bobcat. He never looked for trouble, nor did he back away from it.

He checked up the trail again. A day and a half out of Durango, Colorado and heading north up the Los Pinos river trail in the southwestern corner of the territory. The trail continued to climb beside the small stream.

Jim pulled his low-crowned gray hat down to shade his squinting eyes and stared around the high country with its good evergreen forest cover. He wondered what the altitude was here. The air was crisper now than when he left the 6,505 foot level at Durango. It would be near freezing tonight. The faint trail had been leading upward ever since they left Durango.

Due northwest he could see the Rio Grande Pyramid shouldering its way into the blue sky over the lesser ridges and peaks. He had to be close to the gold camp. The 13,800 foot mountain had been his guidepoint most of the trip. The Los Pinos River had now shrunk in size until it was little more than a bouncing creek, ten to twelve feet wide and never more than two feet deep. No man could drown in that much unless he were unconscious or held under.

A gust of wind brought a new smell to Jim Steel, causing him to kick the sides of his long time mount, prodding him forward. Jim's wilderness-trained nose caught a touch of smoke in the air and it was tinged delightfully with the unmistakable smell of frying venison. He had to be close to the camp, and the gold strike.

Around the next bend in the rough-hewn excuse of a trail a small canyon opened. It struggled to be a quarter of a mile long, and a gush of misshapen haphazard tents blossomed on the near side of the stream. Jim guessed there were thirty tents extending to the middle of the canyon. At the near end of the trail he

5

spotted a square log cabin, nearly finished. It lacked only a roof. Two men still worked on it as Jim rode by.

Smoke spiraled upwards from a dozen wood cooking fires. There were less than two hours of daylight left, and it was almost supper time. But only a few men slouched around the fires, and no one worked the sluice boses or panned in the water. That was strange.

Jim saw the reason when he turned his head a moment later. A little above the camp on a shelf of land a big pine stood, and clustered around it were most of the miners from the camp. A flatbed wagon seemed to be the center of attention. On the wagon sat three men wearing suit coats and shirts making it as formal an occasion as any mining camp had ever seen. At the end of the wagon platform stood a young man.

Jim walked Hamlet up the incline and waved his six-gun at two short thin men who tried to grab a sack off Grouchy. He was about to throw a .44 slug past them when they gave up.

No one on the slope paid any attention to him. Jim tied Hamlet to a small pine twenty feet from the wagon and leaned back in his saddle watching the action at the wagon. Soon he swung down.

The three men in suitcoats sitting in sapling-built chairs looked middle-aged and sober-faced. Jim could see now that the youth who stood on the wagon had his hands tied.

6

A miner's court, Jim decided and kept watching his pack mule from time to time. The center judge stood and pointed at the prisoner.

'Josh Ridgely, this here court duly constituted by the Devil's Gulch Mining District, just found you guilty of claim-jumping and cold-blooded murder. Sentence is death by hanging. You got anything to say, son?'

The accused man's eyes seemed strangely calm. As he scanned the crowd his face began to work and soon he appeared to be on the verge of tears. 'He done said it'd be okay to hit the man, just a joke. Fun. Said it wouldn't hurt noway, and he said he'd be nice to me, take care of me since I got no pa. I only did it cause he told me to. He was older'n me. Supposed to honor thy father and older folks. I didn't mean to hurt him, honest, mister.'

'That's what you told us during the trial, Josh. Why don't you point out this here man who told you to do all this?'

Josh looked around the crowd again. 'He just done told me to do it. Don't rightly know his name. He ain't here now. He was a little man. I just got to camp day 'fore that with my pa. Pa got kicked bad by our mule out on the trail, and I figured you'd have a doc here. But Pa died 'fore we got in. Man said fer me to hit the old guy and he'd give me a loaf of bread. Think of that, a whole loaf of bread!'

'Son, you got to tell us what he looked like,'

the judge said. 'What did this man look like?'

'Don't rightly know his name. He was little, had a beard and talked all funny. He told me to hit the old duck. Sure wish he was here now.'

As the young man talked a tall miner with a red kerchief around his neck moved behind the wagon and threw a rope over a sturdy limb on the pine. On the business end hung a 13-loop hangman's knot. Another man backed a heavy dray horse over the wagon's tongue and hitched him to the rig. A moment later they were ready.

'Son, you know you got to die. We got our Miner's District set up here and in the absence of any other law enforcing group, we are the rightful and legal unit of law. That's all 'cording to the laws of the Territory of Colorado. This court is the law here, son. You understand all that?'

'Reckon so, if'n you say, you being older, 'n all. Never meant to hurt old Ben none.' He wiped his eyes and tried to smile again. He closed his eyes, standing there relaxed, calm, not fighting for his life as most men do.

Jim furrowed his brow slightly as the noose came down over the man's head. He watched as it cinched tight and the slack pulled up at the tree trunk where the half-inch rope had been tied. Jim had a feeling about the boy-man. He was a half-wit, and somebody had used him. But a Miner's District death sentence was binding and legal in nearly every state and territory around. He had to let it stand.

In any place that ten miners got together they could form a legal 'mining district.' They elected a chairman and a recorder and thereby became a legal government. Wherever there wasn't any other government they held total sway over mining affairs and civil matters. They made their own laws and rules for staking claims, how big they would be and how many a man might stake. It had worked out in practice very well since the wild days of the California 49'er gold rush.

The three men in suit coats stepped off the flat bed wagon and the taller one nodded at the miner near the horses. The reins cracked down hard on the mare's broad back, the gray lunged ahead jolting Josh Ridgely off the end of the wagon. The big rope knot snapped his head sideways breaking his neck when he hit the end of the rope.

He dangled there, his feet a yard off the ground, spinning slowly around, his head almost on his shoulder, green eyes wide open, glazed, staring straight ahead. His feet kicked twice convulsively, his tied hands thrashed for a moment, then a soft sigh came from his lungs and his crotch turned dark with wetness.

'The body will hang right there for twenty-four hours. Little warning for us that we don't allow no murder in our camp, not even by some half-wit kid. As Chairman of the Miner's District, it's my job to carry out our laws. Any

9

violence in this camp will be dealt with swiftly and sentence carried out at once.'

He looked at the other men who had sat on the wagon with him.

'Mr. Recorder, do we have any further business?'

'Yes, sir. A charge by Murphy against Landers. Murphy accuses this here Landers of claim-jumping.'

The three men in suit coats mounted the wagon again in its new location forty feet from the pine where the lunging gray had been stopped. The two disputants jumped up with them and the tallest judge looked at a pad of paper.

'Mr. Murphy, you accused Mr. Landers of stealing your claim, disrupting your posted corner markers, and filing on your land.'

'Yessir, he shore done that.'

'Mr. Murphy, the committee has investigated the facts, we have talked to both of you concerning this dispute and we have walked over the land involved. It is the findin' of this court that there indeed has not been any claim-jumping. We award the dispute to Mr. Landers as the lawful owner of said claim and his recording of said land so stands.'

Murphy, a tall man with a sandy beard and blond hair, seemed shocked by the announcement. He shook his head. 'No, by God! He stole it! He broke my spectacles and then stole my claim. He moved my stakes and I couldn't see them right. He tricked me and stole my claim!'

Landers, the winner in the dispute, jumped down from the wagon shaking hands with his friends who crowded around.

Jim loosened the cinch on Hamlet and watched the ex-actor bounce his head in agreement before he reached for more grass.

When Jim looked back at the wagon, Murphy had pulled his sixgun and fired at the miner's committee. One man fell off the wagon and Murphy kept blazing away. Before Jim could react a dozen shots boomed from the crowd and Murphy slammed over the far edge of the wagon with five lead slugs in his heart.

'Meeting adjourned!' Somebody yelled and the group broke up, a few pausing to watch the lifeless body hanging from the pine. Others looked at the three men in suit coats. One was dead, the tall man who read the verdict was only slightly wounded.

The two dead men were dragged to a pit at one side of the camp and rolled into it. Volunteers began shoveling a foot of dirt over the new corpses.

Jim watched and decided law and order in this mining camp were about average. As he untied Hamlet from the tree, Jim saw a small man on the other side of sixty shambling toward him.

'Howdy, tall man, how'd you like that for justice?'

The man was older than Jim had first thought, had a slight limp and carried one shoulder lower than the other. His left hand had been injured so it turned inward and his fingers pointed perpetually toward his wrist. His grin showed ragged, tobacco stained pegs of teeth over a short, white beard.

'The hanging went off smooth enough,' Jim said.

'Yeah, not a hitch. One out of two ain't bad for this place. Harry Stephano, he's the chairman of the district.' The old man chuckled, and Jim could see a glint in his dark eyes. 'Seems as how Harry's gonna have one hell of a time finding a third man to serve on his danged committee now.'

'Mining District law?'

'Right, son. We're forty miles from Durango. This here's even gonna be in another county once it's set up. Anyways the sheriff down at Durango don't care what happens up here, long as we just keep it up here.'

'Sounds normal,' Jim said. 'Any claims open?'

'Yep, plenty, if you want to freeze your rump off in that ice water eight hours a day for dust. But you don't look like no gravel washer to me.'

Jim tried to fathom the old prospector. He was sure he did not know the man. But there was a depth of education and style that seemed to be roughed over and something else ...

12

authority? This man had been somebody who gave orders one day. He was a lot more than what he seemed.

'Stranger, they call me Lucas, Lucas Brace it says on my corner stakes. Got me a little claim down the way there. I'm the camp greeter. Harry asked me to. Sort of my public service work.' His eyes sparkled again. 'We got some rules, like laws. Number one is no killin'. We're damn strict about that. You claim self-defense you got to show two witnesses. For a fair fight you need at least three living witnesses. Rule two is no claim-jumping. We strict about that, too. Outside of them, we ain't got many rules.' He glanced at the mule. 'Stranger, you got much grub on that mule, you better guard it day and night. Food's mite scarce around abouts. Any kind of big game is a day's ride away. Eggs we ain't seen for two months. Bacon we just dream about. Wanta really get rich? Get yourself a wagon and red shirt and teamster grub into this hell hole. That would be a *real* gold mine.'

'Sorry, not me.'

The dark eyes held Jim for a moment. 'Uh huh. But in case you get the urge, I got a wagon.' He looked away, then back at Jim making up his mind. 'Just hope you ain't a lawman. Had one a couple of weeks back. Messed up things terrible. Half the guys here runnin' from something. But sure as rain you don't stake a claim and get panning they'll all

13

think you're a badge toter. Then somebody'll try to stick a knife in your heart some dark of the moon night.'

Jim shrugged, looked over the strip of creek where the miners were back at work. 'So which way is the pay dirt, up or downstream?'

The small man shrugged. 'Up's better, less water to mess with.'

Jim led Hamlet and the mule away past the wagon and up the creek, dodging tents and claim stakes as he went. Just around the bend in the stream he found two free claim-sized chunks of creek and stopped. One spot was as good as the next if this were like the other panning operations he'd seen. He ground tied the buckskin and cut down two small pine trees to cut out his six-foot long stakes at least five inches square. Then he paced off the fifty feet each way, straddling the stream. It would at least look like he were serious. That's when he remembered he didn't have a pan fit to work in the sand. Once the corner stakes were driven in with a rock, Jim sat down on his claim and let his eyes wander over the land upstream. It was a cardinal rule with free gold that the yellow had to come from somewhere, and he knew dozens of men must have looked up this valley before, wondering where the yellow came from. But the gold dust man was a strange breed. Most wanted the immediate return, that instant yellow dust, and not the work, investment and sweat of a hard rock mine.

14

Jim checked the slopes on both sides of the narrow ravine twice before he caught the flash of what could be an outcropping near a small stream that chattered down the cliff and into the Los Pinos below. It looked like the characteristic upthrust of that geological formation needed for gold. The slanting of the layers of rock could mean a special spot where rocks and hot lava had been pushed upwards thousands of feet from the hot interior of the earth millions of years ago. Yes, the upthrust could be there, and the yellow had to come from somewhere. It was a place to explore. Maybe Ted McIntosh had seen the same signs. It was not over fifty yards from where Jim sat.

He turned and watched the old prospector Lucas Brace come ambling up the side of the stream, a mule in tow, with his belongings packed aboard, including two gold washing pans on the side. Without a word Lucas stopped just downstream from Jim and began driving his claim stakes into the rich soil adjacent to Jim's claim. Five minutes later he splashed across the foot-deep creek and dropped a large pan beside Jim's half-opened pack.

'Figure if'n you plan on lookin' like an honest injun miner, you'd need one of these.' Before Jim could answer Lucas held up his hand. 'Oh, I'll trade you straight and even for some of that grub. Deal?'

The sun was down. Jim built a fire and

15

shared his evening meal with Lucas. Jim fried the last of his bacon from Durango, and gave the old man his last two eggs. They ate pork and beans, fried potatoes and onions and the rest of Jim's hard rolls.

The chill charged through the dusk, quickly adding a nip to the air. Lucas said they were at a little over eight thousand feet there.

'The altitude tends to slow a man down some,' Lucas said. 'Leastwise until you get used to it.'

There was a pause as Jim watched the fire.

'Want me to guard your grub tonight?' Lucas asked.

Jim shook his head and threw some small sticks on the cooking-sized blaze.

As darkness came Jim spread his bedroll, then packed up the rest of the food in the flour sack and lashed it back on the mule. He stretched out and cocked his head on his saddle watching the fire burn down to glowing embers.

'How many men been killed up here so far?'

Lucas chuckled. 'Figured you was law all the time. Nobody kept close track. I got here on the third day, and since then, counting the three today, I make it just over thirty, hung and killed.'

'That's a lot of blood.'

'Yep,' Lucas said, turning dark eyes on Jim. 'But there's dust here, *gold dust*, and that means lust and murder as sure as tarnation.

16

Saw one nugget big as a robin's egg, I did.'

When it was full dark, Jim stomped out the last glow of the fire's coals. 'You stay put, Lucas. I'm taking old Grouchy and the food back into the brush a ways. See you in the morning.'

Jim led the mule with the food and equipment aboard working up the side of the ravine a hundred yards into heavy growth of brush and pine. Satisfied at the distance, Jim stopped, tied the mule to a tree and spread out his bedroll. He tried to see the stars but the timber was too thick. Jim turned over and went to sleep at once. If anyone came within fifty yards of him in the dense growth he would hear them and awaken instantly.

Just before dawn, Jim woke and led the mule back to the claim at the river. He stretched out on his blanket for a moment, then changed his mind and built a fire. He could see the fringes of frost on the grass as dawn brought faint light. The placer miners would be breaking ice on the water before long if they continued to pan for gold up here.

In the half-light of dawn, Jim studied the outcropping again, just upstream. It seemed to have the favorable signs. He couldn't wait to go up and check it, but he'd have to go slow. Finding a mother lode is always a chancy proposition. There might be a dozen of them all contributing to the placer. Or a single lode might have been all washed out by now. A

17

hundred factors could confuse and frustrate the hard-rock man looking for the origin of all this free gold in the stream.

Jim was thinking about it too hard and when he heard a noise behind him, he accepted it as Lucas starting to get up. The sound came closer and when Jim turned to check, the only thing he saw were the twin, ugly, black holes of a shotgun's two muzzles wavering less than six feet from his face. There was no time to draw his Centennial Army .44 in the holster tied low on his hip. Lucas still lay in his blankets, snoring softly.

A pair of small, bloodshot eyes grinned at Jim over the black beard and a cigarette drooped from thin lips.

'Steady there, stranger. Steady and y'all gonna stay in one chuck for longer. You lay right still and then old Betsy here ain't gonna do no talking and blow your head off. Y'all gonna live one hell of a lot longer that way.'

CHAPTER TWO

THE BROKEN ARM WARNING

'What the hell you doing?' Jim asked the man with the gun.

'What the hell it look like? I'm gonna have me that there grub you got stashed on your

18

dumbassed mule.'

'You'll get yourself hung.'

'Oh, no suh! Not in Devil's Gulch district. We got just two laws, murder and claim-jumpin'. Y'all got to learn that we got no law 'gainst robbery. Possession hereabouts, friend, is one-hundred percent of the law.'

He kept the shotgun on Jim as he backed toward the mule.

'Been waitin' half the damn night for y'all to get back. Knew couldn't no way sneak up on you in them brush woods. But down here, now that's a different mess of greens.'

Jim knew there was no way he could beat the young man, not against an aimed and cocked double-barreled shotgun. The robber could blast both himself and Lucas in half a second. From time to time the stranger looked over at Lucas who was still rolled up in his blankets, not even his head showing.

'Just lay yourself down face to the ground, easy like and spread-eagle so I don't make no mistake and blow you in half. That'd be a certain damn shame cause then I'd have to pack up and ride hell-bent outa here.'

He had the first rope off the back of the mule now, untying the knots that held the sack of food. He knew just what to go for, and Jim decided the gunman had watched the packing the night before. Jim stretched out on the ground as ordered, and as he did he memorized the face, so if he ever saw it again he would know it. There would be time enough later to settle for the food.

The shotgun began getting in the robber's way. He watched Jim, then walked over and carefully removed Jim's Centennial 1860 .44 from his holster. The man lowered the shotgun and moved back toward the mule. Before he got there three muffled shots blazed in the early morning stillness.

Jim jolted up to his knees and saw the robber down on his haunches trying to lift the sixgun, blood spouting from his right arm.

Jim came to his feet in a running surge and dove at the man just as the robber's good left hand grabbed at the revolver. Jim crashed into the bearded man and they rolled, both struggling for the gun. Jim's hard right fist crashed into the black bearded face once, then again and the robber gave a small sigh and passed out.

Steel caught up his unfired .44 and looked around for the source of the shots. Lucas sat up in his blankets, his still-smoking Dixie 1860 army revolver in his hands.

'Sidewinding sneak thief. Man could get plumb hungry with goings-on like that,' Lucas growled.

Jim stood, picked up the shotgun and saw it was primed and loaded. 'He meant business.'

'Always do out here,' Lucas said. 'Food's next to most valuable item we got. Hadda wait until he got clear of your mule for I let go at him. Didn't want to kill the polecat, just knock down your sixgun. Must have winged him with a lucky one.'

Jim checked the unconscious man. He had a small pouch of gold dust under his shirt on a leather thong. Jim cut the thong and took the dust, in partial payment, then looked at the robber's wound. One of the .44 slugs had splattered through the man's right biceps. He wouldn't pan for gold for a long time. Jim slapped him awake.

The robber came back to consciousness with a scream followed by a long moaning roar of pain and frustration. His black eyes found Jim and he exploded in fury.

'You shot me, you bastard! I was just tryin' for a little food.'

'You own a horse?'

The injured man wiped sweat out of his eyes with his left hand. His right arm hung limp in his lap as he sat on the ground. At last he nodded. 'Yeah, I got a horse.'

A dozen curious miners had walked up attracted by the shots and the screams.

'Good,' Jim said. 'Because you're riding out of here, now. You need to take that arm to a doctor.' Jim knelt beside him and stared into his face. 'I want you to remember this day. Don't ever forget it. Never start something you can't finish.' Jim took the man's left arm and holding it by the elbow with one hand and the wrist with the other brought it down sharply

21

across his outstretched knee the way he broke kindling wood.

The robber's forearm bones snapped like dry pine sticks and his gutteral roar of surprise and pain stormed through the clearing for half a minute until he passed out.

'Goddamn!' one of the miners watching whispered.

Lucas raised his eyes and sat up a little straighter on his blanket, surprise and wonder tinging his features.

Jim stood and pointed at one of the miners watching. 'Go get his horse.' The man hesitated. 'Now,' Jim said softly but with all the encouragement of a bullwhip. The man turned and ran toward the main section of camp and the nag.

A pan of water thrown on the robber's face revived him. He screamed again.

'Shut up,' Jim told him. 'You're half dead, you want to try for any closer?' They stared at each other for a moment, then the younger man looked away. 'You don't hurt half as much as you're going to by the time you get to Durango.'

'A doctor, get me a doctor!'

'That's where you're headed, Nogood. You're going to Durango, if you can live long enough to get there.'

The miner came back leading a pinto that had only one good eye and a slash across her rump. She was saddled.

'Put him onboard,' Jim snapped and two men hurried forward, lifted the screaming man and forked his legs over the saddle.

'Now tie him on. We don't want him falling off and have to walk on into Durango.'

'Tie him ...?'

Jim quieted the question with an angry stare. He had taken over total command. 'See if anybody wants to go along and hold his hand on the ride,' Jim said. 'He sure as hell isn't staying around this camp any longer.'

A dozen more men had wandered up looking for diversion, for anything out of the ordinary to break up the monotony of the hard work of placer mining. Some of them had pants wet to the waist already from working in the cold water.

Jim noticed one man who stood at the edge of the crowd watching everything that went on. It was hard to miss the only man there wearing a black suit, white shirt and string tie. The man looked to be about forty-five, had eye glasses and a carefully trimmed Van Dyke beard. He was practically bald. Slender hands moved constantly to his watch pocket, fondled a chain and fob before pulling out a thin gold watch, then put it back, touched his beard, moved on to his tie before they dropped to his pockets and the ritual began again.

The dark, piercing eyes caught all the action and now concentrated on the man who held command. When the robber's horse walked away, led by one of the wet-trousered miners, the man in the suit faded off with the onlookers.

Jim pulled the heavy flour sack off the mule and began getting breakfast. The fire glowed feebly until Jim built it up with light pine bark, working it down to a quick cooking layer of red coals.

'Flapjacks?' Jim asked, looking at Lucas.

It was the first word he had spoken since the crowd had left his claim. The old prospector bobbed his head. When Lucas noticed that Jim didn't see his acceptance he gave a verbal approval, kicked off the blanket and folded it neatly. He began to reload his Dixie sixgun.

'You, ah ... I mean ... you know that Jones with the scatter gun?'

'Never saw him before.'

'So you ... ah ...' Lucas shook his head. 'You broke his arm?'

'Right,' Jim said, busy with the hotcakes. 'Better than blowing off his head. He's young, he might learn.'

'Think he'll ride for Durango?'

'Yep, unless he tries to bushwhack me. He knows what the warning meant.'

'Warning?'

Jim poured out a flapjack in the pan and watched it bubble and steam. He shifted the half-cooked pancake in the skillet, then in one quick double movement, flipped the oval in the air and caught it uncooked side down in the hot

24

tin. Jim smiled to himself, then looked at Lucas. 'My name's Jim Steel and that's Hamlet, my buckskin. I rescued him from a traveling troupe of actors. You already met Grouchy here. Now, you want to eat this flapjack or not?'

Lucas scrambled for his tin plate and fork, accepting the frypan sized pancake with a grin. He sat down on a stump and took a bite of the hotcake. Jim held up a small jar of homemade apple butter and Lucas let out a surprised yelp and licked his lips.

'Son, where you get all these good victuals? I ain't seen me no apple butter in more'n a year now.' He spread a layer of the jam on the hotcake, folded it and ate it like a sandwich. Between bites he scratched in the dirt with a stick.

'That arm thing, Jim. Sure, I've heard about the broken arm warning. But I never saw anybody do it. It's been around since I was a pup, since the first gunslinger had a stand-up shootout and let the other guy go free with just a broken arm. Most folks know about it, even that guy with the shotgun who calls himself Jones knew. I bet a hind leg of a bull moose that Jones won't even think about stopping before he gets all the way to Denver.' Lucas downed the last of his second big hotcake and took a tin cup full of coffee Jim handed him. It was bitter and strong, the way most miners like it.

'Way I figure it, Jim, now you got no place to

hide. Every man-Jack in camp will either stay out of your way or figure out how to kill you.'

Jim fried another hotcake, ate it himself, and made two more and gave one to the old prospector. When the last griddle cakes were gone, along with the rest of the apple butter, Jim offered more coffee to Lucas, then settled back against his saddle watching the sun tinge the tops of the far hills.

'You aim to do any pannin'?' Lucas asked.

Jim nodded. 'Got several things to get done while I'm here. Might as well make the trip pay for itself.' Jim frowned slightly as he looked at the old prospector. 'Now are *you* going to do any panning or do you just sit around nosing into other folk's business?'

Lucas chuckled, got up stiffly and grabbed one of his gold washing pans with his injured hand. 'Tarnation, I just spraddle-legged asked for that kick in the behind. Me, I'm a moss-backed prospector, and I've got the bad knees, crippled up hands and empty purse to prove it.' He stomped off half in anger but mostly with a touch of traveling minstrel show performer, his limp even more exaggerated.

Jim smiled as the old man left. He had been looking up at the outcropping again just down the bank, wondering if it might be part of the mother lode. Not likely, he decided, shook himself, and grabbed the other gravel washing pan and walked down to the bank of the chattering little stream.

26

'You're panning on my side of the line, old man,' Jim said sternly.

'Fer kittenfish sakes!' Lucas growled and splashed over two steps. He squatted and pulled the pan into the cold water, scooping up a quart of sand and gravel from below a riffle, brought the pan to the surface and began swirling the contents, letting the motion of the water in the pan and the current of the stream carry away the light sand and rocks. Any gold dust would be heavier and settle to the bottom.

'Lucas, where can I find the Devil's Gulch Mining District chairman?'

The old man stopped his pan and looked up. 'Halfway through camp on this side. Harry Stephano's his moniker.'

Jim put down the pan, turned and walked downstream, checking his .44 as he moved, making sure it was fully loaded and ready to fire. As he moved he glanced up at the hanging pine and saw the silent form of the dead half-wit turning slowly in the early morning breeze.

Jim asked one miner directions, then spotted the tall man working a sluice box. Three miners had pooled their claims and worked the sluice together, one shoveling sand and gravel from the Los Pinos into an eight-inch wide U-shaped box twelve feet long. It had a dozen shallow cross bars on the bottom to trap the gold dust and nuggets. Part of the stream had been diverted through the box to wash the sand down its length. The stream water was supposed to carry away the worthless sand and leave the gold.

Jim walked up and the man noticed him, left the stream, and came over, his hand out.

'Morning. My name's Harry Stephano. Heard what you did to that scallywag Jones. Good riddance. He rode out of here with a friend about an hour ago. He took his rifle before he left. Don't want him coming back and bushwhacking the whole camp. Your act of sudden justice, sir, was most commendable.'

'Even though you've got no laws against armed robbery?'

Stephano chewed on his lower lip. 'True, quite true. We have to go at this law thing slowly, one step at a time. We picked the worst crimes to start with. You see, we're not trained in the law, and we're not lawmen. But we probably should expand our set of laws to include armed robbery and thieves, help us become more stable, more solid.'

Jim had shaken the man's hand. 'My name's Jim Steel, just came up to look for some yellow. I'm not hunting trouble, but I don't back off from it.'

'That's what the boys tell me, Mr. Steel.'

Jim stood on the bank of the stream, watching the sluice work, aware that half a dozen men listened to the talk. He didn't want that much publicity about his mission. He motioned Stephano closer to him and talked softly.

'Mr. Stephano. I'm also up here looking for a friend of mine, Ted McIntosh. He was here, wasn't he?'

Stephano took his cue from Jim and spoke quietly, just loud enough so Jim could hear him over the chattering of the Los Pinos as it charged along, bouncing over the rocks.

'Don't remember names much. Can tell you for sure though that we never hung anybody by that name. Keep records on that.'

Jim described Ted McIntosh and the tall man's face brightened.

'Oh, the big redhead, yes, I remember him. But he got himself killed in an accident. Drowned the way I heard it.'

'Bullshit!'

Stephano's head snapped up in surprise. Jim handed him the piece of newspaper he had brought from Denver. The chairman read it, then shook his head. 'Now that I study on it some, does seem strange that a big guy like McIntosh would let a little sluice box hold him underwater.' He paused. 'And you feel the same way, that's why you're here, to find out how Mr. McIntosh really died?'

Jim nodded. 'You remember anything else about it?'

Stephano looked upstream, then shook his head. 'It was up there somewhere near the bend. The committee didn't even go and look at the spot. Two miners said they found him under a tipped over sluice one morning just at

29

dawn. Evidently he'd been there most of the night. Nothing we could do for him, so we buried him and got back to work.'

Jim got the name of the miner who was still in camp who had found the body. The other miner had moved on. He would have a quiet talk with the remaining men very soon.

It would be simple to kill a man and put him in the water and make it look like a drowning. Now his job was to find out who might have done it, and why.

Jim stared at the racing water for a moment hating the glittering gold dust it contained because it had cost the life of his friend. He glanced at the tall man's face. 'I'd appreciate it if you don't let anyone else know why I talked to you. You might tell them I was reporting the attempted armed robbery and asking for a new law.'

They shook hands and Jim wandered on downstream looking over the claims. The sandy bottom gave way to a half-mile stretch of slippery slate sheet rock just at the bend. No gold could accumulate along there. Where the gold panning stopped, a log building stood half-finished. Three men worked around it. Jim guessed it was about twenty feet square. The men had just pulled a log up, then tried to fit it into the notch but it didn't jibe. A man with an axe enlarged the notch and when they slid the log into place again, it fit. There would be little chinking here, the pine logs were straight and true.

Jim turned, and walked back through camp, this time on the other side of the stream. He noticed one tent farther back from the water than the others and saw the man wearing the suit come out. Through the tent flap Jim spotted a flash of wooden floor and the edge of a table.

'Good morning, sir,' the bald man said. 'Wonderful morning, isn't it?'

Jim stared at him for a few seconds, then said it was indeed a fine day and kept moving past.

'Hold on, sir. We haven't met. I'm H. William Lawson.'

He held out his hand. Jim noticed the long, slender fingers without callouses or scars. Two rings sparkled on the hand. It was a soft, slick gambler's hand which went along with his gambler's suit.

Jim brushed the brim of his low crowned felt hat in a faint salute. 'Name's Jim Steel, I came in yesterday.'

The dark eyes seemed to take inventory of Jim. 'I noticed your arrival during the hanging. Then this morning I saw what a strong-willed way you have. I like men like that. Hard to find these days with everyone trying to get rich quick.'

Jim nodded and kept walking. He'd seen all he needed to. Lawson was a gambler and a smooth talker. He would be more than ready to cheat the miners in a crooked card game to take their dust.

'Good meeting you, Steel. We'll be seeing lots of each other, this is a small camp.'

Jim felt a faint dislike for the man and wondered why. Maybe it was because he had spent his share of time freezing off his tail in streams such as this panning for yellow, and he knew how much work and pain was involved in claiming it.

'Nugget! Nugget!'

The call came loud and clear fifty yards ahead of Jim. Men began running to the spot. By the time Jim walked there, thirty men crowded around watching the lucky panner holding up two gold nuggets the size of cherries.

Jim felt the old itch and walked quickly upstream to where he had dropped his borrowed gold washing pan and waded into the cold water of his claim.

CHAPTER THREE

THE HANGING TIME FIRE

As Jim kept washing the quart of gravel and sand he had brought up, the chill of the water seemed to ease, and by the time he had only heavy sand and a flickering of gold dust in the bottom of his pan, he didn't notice the coldness

32

at all.

The sparks and flecks of gold fascinated him as they had when he first panned ten years ago. Now he expertly shifted the water and grit in his pan, forcing more and more of the lighter material to spill over the slanted edge of the pan.

'Tarnation!'

Jim looked over at Lucas, who stood in the middle of the stream. 'Hit something?' Jim asked.

'Well, fer kittenfish sakes, of course! I don't come out here to wash off my tootsies. Wasn't what I was surprised at. 'Pears as how you do know how to use a pan.' Lucas's eyes twinkled for a moment, then he was head down again, arms moving as he rocked his metal pan back and forth working down to the wet gold dust he knew would be at the bottom.

On his first pan, Jim found a little 'color,' maybe a pinch of wet gold dust. It would take thirty times that much to make an ounce, but once he had an ounce panned it was worth over twenty dollars, $20.67 to be exact. Jim had spent almost fifteen minutes working on the quart of sand. If he really worked hard he might make an ounce a day. That would be two dollars a hour, which was fantastic wages compared to a dollar a day on most unskilled jobs. If he wanted to make more money than that he would have to use a sluice box twenty feet long to multiply his efforts.

Jim scraped the yellow up with his thumbnail from the bottom of the pan and deposited the wet gold in the leather pouch he had taken from the robber. The dust would dry, then he would check the gold again for any sand or tiny rocks.

Jim moved and scraped up his quart of sand from a choice spot just below a two-foot high rock. He hoped the lessened current there might have dropped a good quantity of gold dust over the years. Jim was on his second pan from that place when Lucas splashed over to him. In his palm he held a buckshot-sized gold nugget.

'Not a dang bonanza, Jim, but it's a start.' He let Jim admire it a moment, then slid the tiny gold stone into his own leather pouch.

They worked two more hours. Sometimes they came up with no yellow at all, sometimes nearly a spoonful of the soft yellow metal the Indians called 'squaw rock' because it was totally useless.

More than once Jim's eyes had wandered upstream, and now he discovered two more possible upthrust areas where the exposed top of a mother lode might rest. After dark very soon he'd leave Lucas watching the food and take a quick hike along the stream. What could it hurt? Today he'd established himself as just another gold-hungry miner. Tomorrow he would start to dig into what happened to Ted McIntosh.

When the sun stood overhead both men waded out of the stream for dinner. Jim took off upstream with his Winchester and returned fifteen minutes later with a rabbit all dressed out. He skinned it and let Lucas roast it over a spit for lunch. While they ate, Lucas looked at Jim, a scowl on his grizzled face.

'Tarnation, Jim, I had you all tabbed as a lawman. Sure you ain't a U.S. marshal and just ain't showin' us your badge?'

Jim laughed and threw a rock into the creek. 'Who *you* running from, old man?'

'An old woman, who else? Hell, she don't care now, though. Said she'd be better off without me. Let's see, that was back in thirty-seven, and I ain't seen hide ner bustle of her since.'

'Figgers. I can spot a wife deserter every time,' Jim said, licking the last meat off a rabbit leg. 'Wore a badge for a time down in Arizona, until I found out half the people in town hired me so they could frame me for murder, and the other half of the folks didn't care. I don't need that kind of trouble.'

The old man threw the remains of the rabbit carcass into the brush and wiped his mouth on his sweater sleeve, then settled back to pick his teeth with a wooden splinter he'd sharpened.

''Pears as how to me we got enough trouble as it is. Gold and gambling. You meet our gambler friend yet? Surprised he's the only one in camp. Usually a dozen by this time.'

'We've met.'

'Slick one with the pasteboards, but since we got no laws against cheatin' at poker, he's scot-free.'

After lunch Jim pulled up his claim stakes.

'What in tarnation you doin'?' Lucas asked.

'Moving up where the gold is better. Abandoning this claim and filing on a new one.' Jim made two trips with his mule, Hamlet and the cooking gear, then pounded his stakes in directly under the edge of the cliff where he thought he had spotted the outcropping. He covered the small trickle of water that came down the cliff and hoped it had carried the gold from the lode rock into the Los Pinos. During winter that trickle would be a torrent and could wear down the hardest rock.

His stakes were regulation for the district, five inches square and extending four feet out of the ground. He whittled a flat place on two of the corner stakes and wrote in ink his claim notice:

*This claim, fifty feet by fifty feet, is the duly recorded property of James R. Steel, stakes this 12 day of September, 1876.*

Then he signed it, making it legal and binding. Jim didn't even know who the recorder was but according to most mining district rules he had fifteen days to file it with the elected district's recorder.

36

*     *     *

He had made his fifty feet back toward the cliff
a bit generous, so no one would crowd in
behind him, and so he could control the
portion of the cliff face with upthrust. The
stakes went across to the other side of the
stream. This way he controlled the whole fifty
feet of stream on both banks and the cliff face
as well.

Lucas watched Jim, but stayed where he
was. This was the best claim he'd had on the
stream. He wouldn't leave it until he knew
there was something better.

Jim unloaded the mule, and staked out
Hamlet just off his claim, then settled into the
icy water and worked a pan of sand right below
the little side stream. At once he saw this was
richer sand than that below. He swirled the
water, washing away more and more of the
light material. Soon he spotted several
buckshot-sized irregular nuggets. When he was
through washing away the worthless sand and
gravel, he had nearly a cup of free gold! Jim
worked the dust again but lost very little sand.
He stood on the shore and motioned for Lucas
to come up. Lucas did and looked into the pan.

'Well, I'll be dad-blamed, look at that
yellow. That all what it 'pears to be?'

'From my first panning.'

Lucas turned and without another word
walked as casually as he could with his limp

back down the stream thirty yards to his claim and pulled his stakes. He moved upstream and staked his new claim adjacent to Jim's downstream. Then he went back and brought up his gear.

They both panned. Neither found any sand that yielded quite as much as Jim's first haul, but it was a dozen times better than anything they had worked so far. By the end of the daylight, Jim figured he had put almost two pounds of gold dust into his kit. A good six hundred and fifty dollars in hard cash. As the light faded he stole another look at the top of the sheen of wetness on the cliff. The upthrust weathered by centuries of wind, rain and freezing temperatures, could have worn down to expose a raw vein of pure gold. It could be right behind him, a real hard-rock potential, it just damn well could be! Deep in his pack Jim had a rock hammer. Tomorrow night he'd do a little prospecting. Yes, tomorrow he would pan for more gold as well.

Just before full dark, Jim changed his mind and worked his way up toward the outcropping behind his claim. Before he got there he glanced up and down the stream, but no one in camp paid any attention to him. But as he went higher he had a feeling someone above him was watching. He turned and through a screen of young pines on top of the bluff twenty feet higher, he saw the head and naked torso of an Indian. His long hair had been pulled into one braid, but there was no war paint. Jim made a quick sign of friendship and welcome. It was from the universal sign language of the plains Indians that most tribes understood, but the brave in his twenties, only stared at Jim, than vanished into the woods without a sound.

Jim remembered the features of the Indian, trying to place his tribe. He wasn't the more swarthy Apache. Only the Jicarilla Apache would be this far north even on a long hunt. He could have been a roaming brave from any tribe looking for big game, a hunter ranging far for meat for the hungry ones in his tipi. Jim gave up his look at the lode stones and went back down to the claim to get their supper.

There was a tribe of Ute Indians whose homeland was around this southern corner of Colorado Territory and spilled all over this part of the Rockies. He worked at the fire, making it blaze up to produce the coals he liked for cooking.

There was also a big tribe of Navajo in the upper reaches of New Mexico. He could have been one of them. Of the three tribes only the Jicarilla Apaches were in a nasty mood that fall.

He saw Lucas pull off his boots, drying his feet and legs, putting on dry socks he had spread out during the day in the sun.

'Old bones can't take the wet like they used to,' Lucas said by way of explanation.

39

'Consarnit, don't laugh, whippersnapper. You're gonna be old yourself one day.'

Jim sat down beside Lucas and began massaging the man's lower leg, working on the calf muscles until they warmed and relaxed.

'Kittenfish sakes, that feels good. Where you learn to do that? Should get me a darky kid to do that every day.'

Jim got to the question he'd wanted to ask. 'Ever have any Indian trouble around here?'

'Injuns? Shucks no. Nothing in here they want, and if there was any game, we run it off or shot it. Injuns don't bother us.' He rubbed his legs now and backtracked. 'Oh, we see an Injun now and again, mostly upstream, but they ain't hostile. Used to be some Utes around here. When the Jicarillas come, that's when I pack up and move out fast.'

'Just saw a brave up there on the cliff. He looked like a hunter.'

'Yep, that's what he was. Jist so he don't start huntin' me.'

'They never have attacked the camp?'

'Not so you could notice.' Lucas paused, took out a battered pocket knife, the blade sharp enough to shave with, and began whittling on a stick. 'You ready yet to tell me why you come all the way up here, Jim?'

Steel stifled a grin. Old Lucas was nobody's fool. 'Why not? I hear you've got a mouth tighter than a kid under a quince tree.'

Jim told Lucas his suspicions about the

40

death of Ted McIntosh, and exactly why he was there.

'Well, dadblamed it, Jim. I do remember that McIntosh. Seemed like a nice sort of lad. Worked a claim right down from me for a time, and he did work. Make your belly jump up and say howdy the way that man pulled gold out of the sand. Never caused any trouble. Guess he was here for nearly two weeks 'for he turned up dead that morning. I didn't go down to the place.'

'And you never heard anybody arguing with him, or fighting? Ted wasn't exactly hard to get mad.'

'Nope, far as I saw he was even-tempered, didn't even drink too much out our Saturday night campfires.'

'He have anybody he talked with, like a friend in camp?'

'Not so as I can remember. I didn't wet-nurse him, mind ya.'

Jim pursed his lips, spat on the ground. 'Yeah. Well, just keep this to yourself. Way I figure it is somebody put his head in the creek so they could lift his pouch of dust.'

Lucas rubbed his deformed left wrist, then slowly shook his weather-grained face. 'Yep, you might be right. Mac was here for two weeks, panned most of the time, so say he came up with fifteen ounces of dust. That's about three hundred dollars.' Lucas poked at his black stubs of teeth with the new pick he had

41

whittled. 'Guess there might be several men in a camp this size who would split a head for that kind of cash money. A cow hand on the range works a year for that much.'

Jim thanked the old prospector and turned back to working on the food. Lucas brought up the kind of young pine tree bark that Jim liked for his cooking fire.

'Know this is Saturday night?' Lucas asked.

'It still gets just as cold,' Jim said, pulling his coat around him tighter.

'Not for everybody. Some have a big bonfire going and the pickers and stompers scratch out some music. Usually helps pass the time.'

Jim opened the next to last can of beans and dumped them into his fry pan, edging it half way into the glowing coals.

'And whiskey?'

'Always a dozen bottles or so making the rounds. Ever see a mining camp very long without booze?'

The more Jim thought about it the better it sounded. Tongues would rattle much freer with the aid of a few shots of rotgut.

'Guess I better take in the festivities,' Jim said. 'And if you're there, keep your ears open.'

Just after dark, half a dozen men got the big fire going. It was nearly midway in the camp back on the flat where they laid out the four-foot circle of rocks and built up the fire. Somebody found a pitch stump and dug out the turpentine-saturated heartwood that burned like kerosene. Before long they had a roaring fire, flames jumping three feet high, and soon it grew to be three feet across. Two score men gathered around. Jim and Lucas stood at the fringe of the group.

Soon a fiddler came, tightened his horsehair bow and began scraping out a tune. A banjoman and two mouth organ players filled in one the bandstand and the little campfire rocked to the favorite tunes most of the men hadn't heard since they left 'back home.' More than one eye grew wet.

When the players took time out for offerings from the whiskey bottles, the stories began. They ranged from bear hunt tales to yarns about Indian fighting. Soon the musicians were back at work and the men again were thinking about sweethearts and wives who were back home somewhere.

Most of the men hadn't seen a woman for six months to a year. They rushed from one gold strike to the next, staying around until the color faded to nothing in their pans, then grabbed their horses and rushed off to some new wilderness and some new icy stream. One miner told how he walked thirty miles once just to sit and watch the town's three white housewives walk by as they went shopping. It was a treat long remembered.

Jim knew from experience that women and mining camps didn't mix. It often took years for a mining settlement to shake down and smooth out so someone would risk bringing in a wife and family. Before that happened there often was an organized county or city with a sheriff, deputies and a church. Devil's Gulch camp was less than five weeks old, and it was a long way from being ready for women. It might never be if all that was here was the placer free gold. Now if it had a rock mine...

Jim looked at the miners. Most wore mud-smeared, cheap pants, wool shirts, sweaters and homespun and overcoats. Half had suspenders and slouch hats. Only a dozen or so wore guns. They were the dregs of the West. Fifty men in camp and not more than a handful of them could earn an honest living in any of the towns or on the ranches of the West in that year of 1867. Misfits, thieves, deserters, outlaws and gamblers, all bound together under the Devil's Gulch Mining District code and its two-law system. They would be here until the free gold gave out. Then it would be hell-bent for the next spot where yellow sand flowed down some lost creek high in the mountains.

Chairman of the Mining District, Harry Stephano, stopped the music and stood in front of the fire.

'Men, this here's Saturday night, and come dawn, it'll be the Lord's day. I'll be holding holy services for any of them who wants to come up on the flat by the wagon. I thank you.'

When he stepped down a dozen minors

hooted at him and then laughed at some private joke. A score more men crossed themselves hurriedly. The call came again for the music.

A middle-aged man tottered toward the fire, stopped, turned and as he did a stream of amber fluid sloshed from his whiskey bottle into the fire where it burned with a sharp, searing crackle. The miner blinked at the sudden blaze and faced the men.

'Make a little spee ... spaa ... speech. I'm Willy Bradshaw, and by god, it's my wife's birthday. Drink a little toast ... a little...' He stopped and stared out at the men, then fell forward still trying to form a toast to his wife. Someone caught him and lowered him to the ground, after taking the bottle away from him.

Jim moved deeper into the group, watching everyone and trying to listen. Bradshaw now was sharing his bottle with the others, getting drunker by the minute. So far Jim had learned very little that would help him root out McIntosh's killer. Nothing tonight helped so far. Jones, the man he had chased out of camp that morning had been a good prospect. He had been in on three disputed claims, and when he left had no panning gravel at all. However he still seemed to eat well and had plenty of money and dust, according to Lucas.

Jim felt he was swimming up a river against a strong current. No matter how much he worked, he ended up right back at the starting point. He had heard nothing to give him the faintest clue to Ted's death. What if the man who murdered Ted had moved on the next day?

Jim circulated again, then saw the drunk, Bradshaw, staggering to the front of the men toward the fire. This time he waved an almost full quart of whiskey, singing and shouting. The musicians stopped playing as Bradshaw paused by the fire, weaving. He turned and waved at the crowd.

'By damn, make it ... made it up here,' he said.

The miners cheered.

'Gotta make a little toast...' Bradshaw blinked, turned, then his knees buckled and he fell into the fire, hitting the three-foot high flames with his chest and sending up a storm of sparks. His face and hair were just beyond the flames. His right arm flailed wildly with the bottle of whiskey. Somebody grabbed at him, but a short, thickset man jumped up, drew his sixgun and kicked the hands away.

Bradshaw's right arm came down, the whiskey bottle smashed on a rock, and alcohol flooding half the fire, soaking Bradshaw's sleeve and dropping his arm into the flaming gush of burning whiskey.

Bradshaw screamed as the fire enveloped him. Another miner jumped forward to help Bradshaw, but the man with the gun kicked his legs out from under him and pushed him back into the crowd.

'Christ, Conway, let him out, he's burning to death,' a voice screamed.

'Bastard fell into the fire by hisself, let's see if he can get out by hisself,' Conway shouted. He had a heavy, black beard and powerful shoulders.

'He's burning alive,' someone else shouted.

Bradshaw's tortured screams stopped abruptly as he lost consciousness. Then he came back, his agony spilling out of his mouth. His right arm burned like a gasoline torch, the cloth of the shirt now consumed, his flesh turning black, bubbling, charring as the hungry alcohol-fed flames ate into his tissue. Bradshaw screamed again and lunged away from the fire, but moved only inches.

Conway standing over him hooted, yelling encouragement to Bradshaw: 'Just a little more, fatass, and you'll be out.'

Jim drew his sixgun and blasted two shots into the sky, storming forward, bowling over men as he ran. The square-cut Conway faced him for only a moment before Jim's boot lashed out catching him squarely in the crotch, dumping him over backward with a tormented scream of his own. Jim grabbed Bradshaw's boots and boosted him from the fire, then smothered his arm and the burning clothing with a quickly furnished blanket.

The smell of burning flesh made one man gag and throw up, other strong men turned

47

away. The smell was unlike any Jim knew of, and he had known it too often. Carefully he turned Bradshaw on his back. The right arm was a little more than a blackened pair of bones with shards of flesh attached. Bradshaw's torso was burned horribly, his hair singed and his face blistered and puffing badly. Jim wondered what kept the man alive and conscious. He should be dead from fear and shock alone.

Bradshaw's left hand tugged at Jim's holster and pulled out the .44.

'For God's sake, somebody shoot me,' he screamed.

No one said a word.

'I'm half dead anyway, put me out of my misery!'

No one moved.

'You shoot horses don't you?' he screamed. His words blending into a moaning, agonizing appeal as the pain seared through his body again. Sweat burst out on his puffed face.

'For God's sake, take pity on me!'

The man Jim had crotch-kicked struggled to his knees, his eyes twin daggers of hatred for his attacker. He had dropped his gun. Bradshaw saw Conway and recognized the man.

'Conway, you bastard. You wouldn't let them help me!' Bradshaw screamed, then turned the sixgun and shot twice, blasting two slugs through Conway's chest, killing him instantly.

Still no one moved around the fire.

Bradshaw tried to lift his head where he lay in front of the fire. He screamed again at the effort, bellowed in total agony as his right arm moved. He waved the .44 with his unburned left hand. 'I just killed a man, so hang me! Put me out of my pain. Damnit, execute me, somebody! Stephano, it's your job, kill me for God's sake!'

Harry Stephano turned away, tears streaming down his face. It sounded as if he were mumbling a prayer.

Slowly Bradshaw turned the big gun toward his own temple. Jim knelt beside him, willing the man to pull the trigger, trying to help him. But at the last moment, the hand relaxed and Bradshaw began crying through his pain.

'God, I can't do it. Please somebody, put a bullet through my brain. Shoot me like any busted up cow pony. Kill me now!'

Slowly Jim Steel reached the man's left hand which held the sixgun and lifted it toward Bradshaw's head. The burned man looked at Jim, gratitude in his eyes.

'Thanks,' Bradshaw said.

Jim waited while the man tried to pull the trigger again, but too much of his strength was on the trigger. Quickly Jim jammed his own finger into the trigger guard and the .44 roared, blasting the big slug into Bradshaw's brain, snuffing out his life and ending his suffering.

No one made a sound. No one moved. Then

49

slowly men stood and walked away. Most of them were gone when Harry Stephano came down beside the two bodies and where Jim still knelt. The mining district chairman had out his .45, cocked and leveled at Jim's heart. Tears still ran down his cheeks.

'Don't move, Jim. I'm sorry, but I've got to arrest you for the murder of Willy Bradshaw.'

<br>

CHAPTER FOUR

# HOSTILES OR HUNTERS?

A dozen miners turned back when they saw the confrontation, straggling back in ones and twos until there were twenty men surrounding the two men at the still roaring fire. Most of them looked unhappy, some mumbling veiled threats.

One man with the red suspenders and red shirt of a former teamster shook his head at Stephano.

'What the hell, he didn't kill nobody, Stephano. This gent even pulled old Willy out of the damn fire. Saved his life is what he did. Saved him all that suffering from laying there burning alive. Now how you gonna call that murder?'

Harry Stephano shook his head, but kept the gun aimed at Jim.

'Don't matter what he done before. His finger pushed in there and fired Willy's .44. I saw it. That's what he's charged with. Circumstances don't make no difference in the eyes of the law.' When Stephano finished he wiped his eyes clear of the tears.

A miner wearing a black and yellow mackintosh shook his head. 'Not so, Stephano. This man done pulled Willy out of the fire. Then all he did was turn the gun so Willy could pull the trigger himself. God, man, didn't you see the pain Willy was in, he was burned, sufferin' so I thought for sure he'd pass out again. His one arm was burned so bad you could see the bones. Look at that arm, white bones sooted black. Hell, far as I'm concerned Willy pulled the trigger himself. And I see him do it. Yes sir, I'll swear to that in your court, and I bet all the rest of us here saw the same thing.'

There was a chorus of shouts agreeing with the speaker.

'Look,' Stephano said. 'I know what you're doing. I agree Willy wanted to die, but he had help. And that's illegal and that's killin' and we got a law against that. We got to know the law and live by it or we're all animals. So I still say this man has to be tried for killin'. You want to testify for him, fine with me.'

A small bald-headed man leaning on a makeshift crutch scowled at Harry. He lifted the crutch and pointed it at the committee

51

chairman.

'Old man, you don't know what you're talking about. We saw it. From your position you didn't see it none too good. Yeah, I remember. You were over to the side, had to look right through the man here who moved the gun around for old Willy. No way you could see what he was doing there. So we understand that you made a mistake.'

Another man came up from the back of the group. Jim recognized him as being the remaining member of the miner's committee. He wore a full beard and a brown cap with a bill that he pulled so low it almost hid his eyes. His name was Winslow Carter.

'Harry, I don't think you can hold him. He was helping Willy. And he did save his life, even though it was too late. We all liked Willy, and we know that he wouldn't want nothing like this to happen, specially to the gent who saved his life once. Willy killed himself, Harry. I won't vote to hold this man. Since I'm now fifty percent of the committee, it's a tie vote so it fails. Your motion can't pass.' The man reached out and slowly pushed the muzzle of the big .45 away from Jim.

Harry Stephano sighed. 'This is not an easy job. I knew that when I agreed to take it. We need another member. Any of you want to volunteer?' Nobody said a word. The darkness deepened. 'If any of you want my spot I'll be glad to step down right now.' Again there was

52

only silence.

'All right, I accept the tie vote. Mr. Steel here is certainly no troublemaker, nor is he a killer. We saw what he did to that no-good Jones.' Harry stared at the fire for a full half minute. Then slowly he pushed the .45 back in his holster. 'I ain't saying you're right. A man got killed, and we all know how and why, and according to the strict letter of the law, Mr. Steel is involved. But sometimes we can't make everything work out the way it should. Mr. Steel, I'm withdrawing my charges. I find the death of one Willy Bradshaw came at his own hand. Case closed.'

The miners around cheered, then Harry picked four of them to take the two dead men away and bury them.

'Separate graves for each man,' Harry called. 'I'll be there to read a few words of Christian burial before you cover them.' He turned back to Jim.

'I hope you understand. None of this was intended to be of a personal nature, Mr. Steel. I was only trying to do my duty. If we have no law and order, none of us will live long enough to enjoy any gold we might find here. Security must come first. Security, stability, permanence. There might some day be a town here if the gold holds out long enough.'

'I understand, Mr. Stephano. I was a lawman myself once, and I know your problems.' Jim had seen a small man at the side

53

of the circle as they talked. Now he was gone. He was a midget perhaps. 'Could the short person I just saw now be the "small man" the boy who hung yesterday referred to?' Jim asked.

Harry shook his head. 'That's impossible. That man's name is Mars Duncann. He couldn't possibly have been the man who told Josh to kill the old man. Mars is a mute.'

Jim nodded, watched the bodies of the two men carried away. Will Bradshaw had to be moved in a blanket. Jim turned back toward his end of camp. Lucas had waited until he saw that Jim was not in trouble, then he left.

Jim wandered through the camp. He had seen a dozen like it, hugging creek beds, with the men battling the cold, the wind, and rain as well as the river and the greed and violence of the other miners. But gold fever was a reality for all of these men, and usually incurable.

He walked past tents and small fires where men huddled, trying to stay warm, or drying out boots and socks and pants for work the next day. Most of the miners panned on Sunday.

Jim came around one tent on the makeshift trail along the river and found himself looking into the eyes of the small man he had seen at the fire. Mars Duncann wasn't a midget, he was grotesquely misshapen, a true dwarf, his head too large for his body, his arms long, reaching almost to his ankles. His torso was normal but

54

his legs extremely short. He glared at Jim and made a rumbling sound somewhere deep in his throat. Suddenly he scowled and waved Jim away. He made the motion a dozen times, and then drew a six-inch, thin-bladed knife from his boot and held it with the point aimed at Jim.

Steel spoke then for the first time to him. 'I have no quarrel with you. I am no threat to you, so you have no reason to fear or resent me. I am simply passing by. And you have no need for the knife.' Jim turned his back and walked away and heard no more of the unhappy growling.

As he moved through the tents toward his end of the stream, Jim pondered the dwarf's behavior. He undoubtedly was teased and ridiculed by most of the miners. It would make him wary. His deformity and lack of speech would make him easy prey. But there was nothing to indicate that he might have been the one who urged the dead half-wit boy to kill. The facts all pointed another way, and Jim knew he had no time to pursue them.

Jim was deep in thought as he rounded a tent and for a moment was outlined against a fire burning near the front flap. A pistol shot boomed from the darkness ahead and the bullet whipped past Jim's shoulder as he dove to the right out of the firelight. He lay totally still for a few seconds listening. He could see nothing ahead. Slowly, Jim began to move. As silently as a sidewinder, he slithered to a thick pine tree and stood behind it.

In the darkness he could see little. There were no more campfires in this area. The attacker had planned well. Then Jim heard someone move, a twig cracked, leaves rustled. Jim charged at the sounds. He heard the man yelp in surprise, then came hurried, running steps headed away, moving quickly into the brush up the hill.

There was no way Jim could catch the man. On this cloudless but moonless night he couldn't see a dozen feet in front of him. The man ran and stopped, then crawled noiselessly; when he ran again he was at right angles to his first path and well to one side.

Jim gave up, and on his way back to the trail he kicked something on the ground. He reached down and found a fur-lined cap, with ear flaps that folded down. Jim had seen few like it in camp. He took it with him back to his diggings, and stretched out on his blanket roll facing the small fire Lucas had built, his .44 in his hand.

Lucas nodded as Jim lay down. 'Conway was no loss to mankind,' Lucas said. 'Consarnit, still hurts me some whenever a man dies violently, before his time. But Conway I do't pain for at all. Will Bradshaw now. I pain for him. Bradshaw 'en me did some drinking together on a cold night. Harmless old man, never hurt a gopher even or a crawfish. I've seen him half fall down to keep

56

from stepping on one of them crawdads in the creek. Damn hate to see him go like that. But you did fine, Jim. Nobody expected him to get out of the fire once that bottle of booze broke on him.'

Lucas took a pull from a pint and passed it to Jim. Jim tipped the bottle and took a swallow of the raw whiskey, then passed it back.

Neither said a word for a few minutes. The time stretched out and they both kept staring at the fire.

At last Jim stood, took the cloth sack filled with the remains of his food and his blanket. 'I'll be in the brush again tonight.'

Lucas shook his head. 'No need now, you've got friends. All of Willy's friends are with you. The eight or ten others are scared of you. No jackass dumbbell is gonna tangle with you now.'

'Good, I'll get a fine night's sleep.' Jim left the mule and carried the grub two hundred yards up the slope. There he built a quick mattress of broken off pine branches and stretched. Jim went over the day's events and knew he had done as well as he could expect. Not much progress toward finding out who killed Ted McIntosh, but he was laying the groundwork. It would come.

Before he knew it he drifted off to sleep and woke with a crick in his neck as the first splash of light hit the eastern sky.

When he got back to the campsite Lucas had

already washed out six pans of sand. He came in, cold and wet, and hovered around a fire he had started before he went out. He stood drying and asked Jim if he had any trouble. Jim shook his head and dug into the food sack. When he took out two eggs padded and protected against breaking in a small glass jar, Lucas yelped in delight.

'Land O'Goshen, a real egg. Two of them,' Lucas said reverently. 'I haven't seen an egg in six months. Hey, can I fry them? Been so goldarned long I near forgot how to do it.'

Jim dug out some potatoes and sliced them into the other frying pan with a mess of sliced onions and a lump of bacon grease. By the time the potatoes were done, the eggs were too and they hunkered around the cooking fire and ate. Lucas mopped up the last of the yellow stain of the egg yolk in the tin plate with the potatoes and then drained his coffee cup.

'Now that's what I call a breakfast to kick a body right out into the water and getting to work,' Lucas said.

They both worked half the morning before one miner watched their panning and discovered the heavy yellow they were finding. He quietly staked a claim right below Lucas, and told a friend who moved in below him. Soon a dozen men had staked claims on both sides of the pair. Only those below Lucas and Jim found any yellow. Even so, it was much less per pan than Jim and Lucas were producing.

On the noontime break, Jim went to the Devil's Gulch Miner's Committee recorder and officially filed on his claim. Then he went back and Lucas did the same thing. Now it was all legal and binding.

Both men worked the rest of the afternoon in the cold water. Lucas built a campfire near the stream where several of the men went from time to time to warm chilled hands and feet. Curiously, Jim found himself getting used to the cold. He pulled out almost a pound of gold dust during the hard day's work. He dropped on the grassy bank in the last bit of sunshine and groaned. He wasn't put together to do this type of work for long. But he had established a good solid front and now he could begin to investigate Ted's death. He had squeezed almost $300 worth of gold from the cold water today, and he'd see that Ted's widow got that when this was all over.

Jim took the gold with the other he had and carried it to a new hiding spot in the woods. He drifted deeper into the woods than he had been before and up the gentle slope of the mountain. Once he backtracked to see if anyone was following him, but saw nor heard no one. When he was sure he was alone, he found a lightning-split pine and paced off six steps to the north. There under a four foot pine tree he dug a hole. Over the hole he put a slab of rock, then put the gold dust inside and recovered it.

59

Over the rock he put dirt and pine needles and leaves until it looked like the rest of the ground.

After walking fifty yards back toward camp, Jim sat down against a tree and watched both his new cache and the trail. It was almost dusk when he decided no one was watching, and he went back to camp. There he picked up his rock hammer and crossed the stream. He watched for a moment, but none of the miners were interested in his movements. No one cared. He slid into the brush on the other side and began working his way up the incline toward the sixty-foot bluff that fronted his claim. He climbed steadily through the brush and up the rocky slope until at last he was on top. He could look directly down on his own claim now. As he looked around he realized he was standing directly at the point where he figured the mother lode might be, the outcropping. He took a better look and realized it was not a true outcropping at all, no sudden upthrust had powered basalt and molten rock upward at this point. It was simply a few slabs of fallen rock that had lodged there and not worn down as quickly as the surrounding soil.

Before he could leave the spot to move toward the next potential mother lode location, he sensed movement across from him. Twenty feet away across the small baldness of the cliff he saw three Indians. They wore hunting costumes, two in loincloths and buckskin shirts, the other, an older Indian with long hair, wore both pants and shirt of buckskin. Each brave carried a strung bow and three arrows in his other hand.

The three red men stood still, then the older one made the sign for 'friend' that Jim had used before. Jim repeated the sign. The older Indian motioned behind him and the younger braves sat down. The long hair came slowly, his palm up, his bow and arrow both in his left hand carried at his side. He came in peace. The Indian wanted to parley.

Jim held his hand well away from the .44 at his side and began walking slowly toward the brave he decided must be a Ute chief or a medicine man.

## CHAPTER FIVE

# GRUB WAGON YONDER

Jim stopped ten feet from the Indian. Now he could see some of the marks of rank on the older man, the one four-inch high braid wrapped with rawhide and sticking straight up at the back of his head with a single brown spotted eagle feather in it; the decorated and beaded sash draped around his neck, a trail of bright beads tied to the high braid and hung over his ear and fastened to a small fur pouch on his shoulder. He was a genuine Ute chief.

The chief stopped when Jim did, made the sign for peace again, and slowly used a dozen sign language motions. Jim didn't know them all, but the clenched fist in front of the chest and moved downward sharply indicated 'to be' or 'to remain.' A wave of the palm at the sky was a sign for the Great Spirit, and quickly Jim got the idea. Then a raised fist with palm outward and the hand moved so the fist opened and the fingers pointed down at the ground. That meant 'bad' or taboo or in some cases 'bad for you.' Now Jim had the message. The bluff where he stood was bad for him and for all whites. It was sacred ground since this was the burial place for his band of roving Ute Indians. The bluff contained the bones of the tribe and probably those of Ute Indian chiefs for hundreds of years and must not be violated by the whites.

When Jim was sure he understood the message he sat down cross-legged and motioned for the old Indian to sit as well. The elderly Indian sat with difficulty, embarrassed by his lack of muscular ability, but the look passed and Jim began using sign language slowly telling the chief that he understood, and that the white men would be told to stay away from the bluff.

Jim repeated the message twice, and the old chief nodded and pointed to himself, then to his forehead. He understood. Jim watched the

Indian. He was Ute for sure, with long black hair, covering his ears, touching his shoulders. It was now streaked with gray. He had a heavy mustache whose untrimmed ends hung below his chin. He had no other beard. Both his hair and mustache had been rubbed with bear grease until they glistened. His eyes were wide-set and black, half hidden by lowered lids. The chief's lips were now held firmly together in a hard line and his nose showed where it had been broken. The chief's hands were strong, with long fingers and broken nails.

Jim waited and soon the old chief started a new message. Jim had to guess at some of the signs. He showed his confusion and the chief began again, using different gestures, pointing to his two young companions. At last Jim got the point. It might be hard to control the young bucks in the tribe if the whites violated the sacred burial grounds. He as chief would try, but he was an old man, slow of foot.

Jim nodded his understanding and said again with sign language that he would warn the whites, and he would not come up here again. The chief seemed satisfied. Jim felt if they had a pipe they could smoke it. Darkness was near.

Jim knew that he should have a present for the old chief. Even though he had not asked for the parley, it was customary. He reached in his pocket and found the jackknife. It was expendable. He took it carefully and presented it to the chief, showing him how it snapped open and then closed. The old warrior was delighted, but showed it only with a glint in his eyes.

There was no doubt in Jim's mind that the old chief would have a present for him. A chief asking to talk would have something to give. The old chief stood slowly now, and thrust his bow and three arrows toward Jim. It was a valuable gift, and much more important than it seemed. He was still a hunter, and a hunter without his bow brought back no game and his family did not eat. To give up a hunting bow and arrows was a royal tribute. Jim thanked him with his eyes, showed the proper awe and surprise. He made the sign for friend once more, then turned abruptly, offering his back to the warriors as proof of his trust, and walked down the bluff in the darkness to the creek. When Jim splashed across the water and walked to the campfire, he saw that Lucas was still working on their supper.

He briefed Lucas on the development with the Utes, then went to see the chairman of the miner's committee. Harry Stephano sat roasting a rabbit over his small cooking fire when Jim found him. Jim explained in detail what he had learned from the Ute chief, and produced the bow and arrows as proof of his contact.

'That's about the size of it, Harry. I'd say these are not war party hostiles, but they could go get plenty of men if they want to.'

Harry harumphed. 'A bunch of dad-blamed, super nonsense!' Harry thundered. 'God almighty has no time for these savages. He won't hold with none of their superstitions and neither will I. It's all a bunch of nonsense, the taboo burial grounds. I won't hear of it. If I want to go up there, I'll damn well go!'

Jim stared at him in surprise. 'The chief would use the same terms about the nonsense of your Christianity, Harry. I'm not asking you to believe what he believes. But I respect his beliefs—and his ability to put an arrow through my heart if I violate any of his territory up there. What should be done is to issue a warning to the men. Tell them that this is Ute hunting land and that the bluff is sacred, a burial ground that is taboo to whites. Most of these men have been around the West long enough to know what that means. It's simply dangerous to go up there and nobody should dig or cut trees or brush or anything on top. I'm not even sure how the Utes bury their dead. They might tie them on poles, or fasten them in the crotch of a tree, or hide them in a cave. What I'm saying is that none of the miners should go up there, and they should know about the danger.'

Harry sighed. 'Damned heathens. They are damned by the Lord God Almighty!' He turned the rabbit on the spit and watched the juices drip into the coals below. 'But what you

65

say is still reasonable. No use stirring up a hornet's nest. I'll get to every campfire, you won't have to worry about that. The filthy heathens! Why don't they mind their own business?'

'Mr. Stephano, it would seem that this is their business.' Jim thanked the chairman and got back to his own campfire in time to salvage part of the stew that Lucas had been working on for half the afternoon between pannings. It was 'goldern' stew. Years ago Jim had learned the term when a rugged cattle drive cook had called it that. One rider asked what that meant, and the cook said it was 'goldern' stew because he was 'golderned' if he knew what all he put in it. Before he finished his second tin plate full Jim discovered slabs of venison, pieces of rabbit and good portions of pheasant.

'Got me that pheasant less than two hours ago when you were out galavanting around,' Lucas said. 'Always have been partial to them tasty birds.'

After the meal Jim made another circuit of the campfires. Halfway around he found a man who wore a coat with a fur-lined collar that matched the cap Jim had found the night before. Jim held the cap out and the man started to reach for it.

Jim pulled it away. 'Is this yours?' Jim asked.

'Could be,' the man said. He was about twenty, slight and tall with that Texan stamp all over him. His soft blue eyes were watery and

66

he sniffled before he spoke again. He looked at the cap, then he shifted his glance up at Jim and pulled his hand back.

'Nope, don't look like mine atall,' he said. The words came out soft and Texan drawled. Jim didn't believe him.

'It matched your coat. Same fur on the collar. Thought you might have lost it last night.'

'You find it?'

'Yep, on the little trail upstream.'

'I never go up that way.'

'Seems to me I've seen you up there. Last night, matter of fact, just after the big campfire.'

'Not me. No suh. I was right here with my friends. We had a bottle we was working on.'

He was lying, but it wouldn't do Jim any good to press it right now and he knew it. He might ask the men around if the hat were this tall Texan's. But after an exchange like this they would close in behind him and say whatever he did. Roughing it this way produced quick friendship.

Jim tossed the cap to the man who caught it. 'I hear your name is Underhill. My suggestion to you, Mr. Underhill, is not to lose your hat again. And if you do, to do one hell of a lot better shooting than you did last night. I know this is your hat, and I know where and why you lost it. I don't take to people shooting at me, especially bushwhacking in the dark. I'm not

67

through with you yet, you remember that, remember it good.' Jim glared at the young man for a full minute, then turned his back on him contemptuously and walked away.

Jim moved on through the camp toward the big bonfire that someone had started again. It was in the same ring where it had burned Saturday night. As he neared the gambler's tent, Jim heard a shout.

'The grub wagon's coming!'

The words spread from fire to fire and soon two dozen hungry miners each with a poke of gold dust and a lantern were running for the log cabin that had been built at the last place where the trail was wide enough for a wagon. The cabin was nearly finished, with everything up but the roof. The walls were solid and chinked with two windows and a door in place. Even the pole rafters were nailed up.

The owner, Abe Lindstrom, had ridden out to meet the wagon. It had been due at noon someone said, and now, eight hours late, it pulled up to the door of the unopened Devil's Gulch General Store.

Jim had run along with the other men. He'd seen supply wagons such as this come into other mining camps, and seen them torn apart before the hapless store owners knew they had arrived.

The team came to a stop trembling from the long pull, sweat staining their backs and the harness. The driver tied the reins, set the brake and jumped down. Then Jim looked at the back of the open wagon. Two men sat on a canvas over the merchandise, and each man held a double-barreled shotgun. Just then one of the scatterguns fired and everyone ducked for cover.

## CHAPTER SIX

## THE THOUSAND DOLLAR SURPRISE

'Git back you damn vultures or I'll blast everyone of you out of your boots!' The man talking had just sent a load of buckshot over the miners' heads and as he yelled he smoothly loaded a new round in the barrel of the double-whammer. 'Go on, git! Nothing goes on sale until tomorrow. Now vamoose or I'll start cutting a swath through you big enough to drive a team of six!' To punctuate his order he fired a second round from the scatter gun and by then all the men began backing up.

'You bring any tobacco?' one man shouted.

'How about some good corn whiskey?' another voice asked.

'Hell, no, you sand washers, we got everything else in here except that whiskey,' the man on top shouted. 'Store'll be open at eight o'clock in the morning. Bring in your dust. That's all we take now is dust and gold coins.

No damn paper.'

Jim sauntered back toward his fire and Lucas fell in step beside him.

'That old galoot is called Abe Lindstrom. He's bound to be the only man who comes out of Devil's Gulch a dime to the good. Mark my words. I told you to quit this playing in the water with a saucepan and get to hauling freight. You any idea what a new pair of boots is going to cost in that store of Abe's?'

Jim said he didn't.

'Lord only knows. Abe will kick it as high as he thinks he can get away with. Knee high rubber boots will be going for at least fifteen dollars. That's for a good two-dollar pair of boots. He's got no competition. Land sakes, Jim. Shore wish you'd had the sense to drive in some wagons of goods. We could have been rich.'

'Lucas, do you remember any of the men Ted McIntosh worked with? Did he make any friends here?'

'Him again, huh? Well, let me see. He did his panning up our way on the creek. Not as high as we are. I kin point out one campfire where he spent most of his time.'

'Let's stop by right now,' Jim said.

'Now? For kittenfish sakes! Goldern, but you got a way with you, Jim Steel. You do get things done. Hell's bells, why not? The guy is called Johnson, Johnny Johnson.' They walked another fifty feet through the camp and then Lucas stopped by a small campfire behind a huge fallen pine and set well back from the stream. One man lounged near the fire finishing a dinner of fresh trout.

'Tarnation, Johnson! Where in blazes did you catch them?'

Johnson was a man in his late fifties. He had only three teeth showing in the front of his mouth and one of them was broken and blackened. He grinned and then laughed.

'Damned if I'm going to tell you, Lucas. You'd find out my hole. I went downstream, you idiot. Think any self-respecting rainbow trout would swim in this murky water?'

'Nope, don't reckon,' Lucas said. He hunkered down next to the fire where he warmed his hands. Then he pointed behind him. 'Friend of mine, Johnson. His name's Jim Steel.'

Johnson stood smiling and held out his hand. 'Yeah, I been wanting to shake you by the hand, partner. You did us all a favor by running that damned Jones character out of camp. But he's a dirty mean bastard, so always watch your back.'

Jim took the hand. At once he liked Johnson. His eyes held a four-square honesty a man could count on.

'Thanks, Mr. Johnson. Could I borrow part of your fire?'

The older man waved and both sat down in front of the flames.

71

'I understand you knew a man named Ted McIntosh,' Jim said.

'Yep. Never believed he drowned, noways. But couldn't prove it. Knowed Ted pretty good. We cooked together for two weeks. He knew gold panning, but he said he was really a hard-rock man.'

'I knew Ted for ten years,' Jim said. 'He could outswim a mad beaver and outfight a grizzly bear. I think he was murdered, but I don't know why and I sure don't know who did it. That's why I'm here.'

'Help you all I can,' Johnson said. 'I still got his poke. He traveled light. Said if something did happen to him, there'd probably be somebody around asking questions.'

'So he knew somebody was after his scalp?'

'Might be. Want his things?'

'Know what's in the bag? Anything that might give us some ideas who killed him?'

'Doubtful. I never really looked through it.'

Jim nodded and the older man went into his wall tent and came back a minute later with a small carpet bag of green and brown. He put it in front of Jim.

'It's all yours, friend. To tell you true, I kind of didn't know what to do with it. He never mentioned any kin.'

Jim took the things out one by one in the firelight and laid them in a stack. He folded pairs of socks. Then he put a dime Western novel on top of the stack. Next he found a .44

72

revolver and a gunbelt. None of the loops on the belt had the .44 rounds in them. Did that mean he had used them up in emergency? The newspaper package he removed next was small, maybe four by seven inches. Jim untied the string and opened it. A sheaf of paper currency spilled out. Jim looked at the money in surprise.

'Well, I'll be damned!' Johnny Johnson said. 'I knowed somebody went through Ted's gear the night he was killed. The next morning after he died I could tell some varmint had been around. Know Ted kept some gold dust in his poke and it was gone. He showed me where he planted the rest of his gold dust and when I went there to look for it, it was stole, too. Looked like somebody with a shovel had moved some dirt and found it. But the coyotes missed the paper money. I'll be damned!'

The bills were all there. Jim counted them in stacks of ten and came up with a dozen.

'Lord God Almight,' Johnson breathed. 'Twelve hundred dollars in cash money I been kicking around under foot.'

'You better stash the bills away with your own dust,' Jim said.

'Why? Ain't my money. Belongs to the kin of McIntosh. Didn't he have a wife somewhere?'

Jim frowned, remembering. The death notice in the paper hadn't mentioned any family. It had said 'friends.' But he hadn't seen Ted for three years. He could have taken a

73

wife.

'As far as I know, Ted hadn't married. If he did and we can find the widow, we'll give her the money. If not, it's yours. Now, stash it with your gold dust before anybody else sees it!'

Jim had repackaged the twelve hundred dollars and tied it securely. Johnson wrapped the bundle again with the tail of an old poncho to keep the bills dry, then he winked at Jim and slid off into the darkness. He came back fifteen minutes later.

'If the gophers around here knew where to dig, they could be the richest varmints in the world. Must be fifty pokes buried out there in them woods.'

'Safe as the bank of Denver,' Jim said. He stared at Johnny Johnson. 'Ted say what he was up to? You see, Ted had never panned any gold before that I know of. He was a hard-rock man, a tunnel and shaft expert. What was he doing on this little creek with a gold pan in his hands?'

'He panned gold good, fact is he showed me a wrinkle or two. After he got a stake he played a lot of poker, more toward the last,' Johnny said.

'With the camp gambler?'

'Yep. First two weeks or so he panned, and then in the afternoons he vanished for three or four hours. I remember one night he came back just after dark with a rabbit he'd shot, and he had a grin as big as a full blown moon on his

Irish face. He didn't say a word, but I figured he'd found something. Just what I don't know.'

Jim looked up quickly. 'And after that he spent more time gambling and less time in the woods?'

'Yep, how'd you know?'

'Just a guess. He say why he was playing cards?'

'Once he said he was going to need a good bit of money shortly. Cash money or dust, that's what he said he'd be needing. I offered him my dust, but he just chuckled and said he had to have big money, maybe ten thousand dollars.'

Jim took the rest of the gear from the duffel bag. Another pair of socks and an old family Bible with the edges all worn and bent, and a small rock hammer.

Johnson's face lit up when he saw the hammer. 'Now that was one of the things I teased Ted about. Told him he must be a damn good carpenter to be able to hit nails with that funny looking little hammer. Never did tell me what it was for. He'd just grin and laugh and say that little hammer might make him a million dollars. He took it with him on his hikes, but then at the last he didn't use it much, he was playing cards more than anything else, then, even during the day.'

Jim stood and the other two men did as well. He held the Bible and the rock hammer.

'Johnny, I want to take these, the rest of the

things you might as well use. And keep that bundle hidden until I find out about any kin. I'd appreciate it if you didn't mention this to anyone, especially my asking about Ted. I don't want to scare off the killers.'

Johnny nodded. 'Sure enough, Jim. You can count on me. Anybody who can cook with an old reprobate like Lucas here, must have a heart of pure gold and a cast iron stomach.' He slapped Lucas on the shoulder and the two men laughed at each other as Jim turned back up the trail toward the last embers of their campfire.

Jim pulled a gold filled watch from his pocket. He snapped open the fancy hunting case and checked the time. It was 9:15. The watch was one of Jim's few luxuries. A genuine 23-jewel Railway Hampden, adjusted, that had cost him forty two dollars in San Francisco. It was the finest timepiece made. Never before had he owned a watch that cost more than five dollars.

Lucas put a few sticks on the fire and sat watching Jim.

'This is important to you, isn't it, Jim? This finding your friend's killers?'

'Yes, that's the only reason I'm here.' He sat still then and stared into the fire, watching the hungry coals claim one small stick after another. Jim was working over piece by piece the new information he had about Ted.

Ted went hiking in the afternoons. Why?

Was he looking for the mother lode? A hard-rock man's mind would automatically think that way. When he suddenly changed his pattern, stopped looking for it, it could mean he had found it. Then he needed money, big money. That could only mean that he had found the mother lode, thought that it was worth developing, and now needed only the money to start work on the site, hire men, put up a stamping mill, and get the ore out of the ground.

So Ted McIntosh had found the mother lode, then began gambling to get the money he needed. From there on anything could have happened. He might have caught the gambler cheating and been slugged from behind, then downed. He might have won too much money from the gambler. The slick man might have hired someone to kill Ted so he could get back the money.

But did anyone else know about or even suspect the mother lode? Certainly not the gambler. He couldn't care less about digging holes in the ground. Still the gambler seemed to be one of the keys to the problem. He had to know more about this gambling man. Jim stood and flipped a double-eagle piece into the air and caught it.

'I think I'll go over and see if the gambling tent is crowded tonight.'

Lucas looked up from the fire. 'He cheats, you know.'

77

'All gamblers cheat, I want to see how good he is at it.'

'And you'd gamble a month's wages to find out?' Lucas asked.

'Yes, when ten thousand or a hundred thousand dollars might be at stake.'

Lucas sat up straighter. 'A hundred thousand...' His voice trailed off. 'I don't wanta know about it. Good hunting.'

Most of the miners' fires were out and their tent flaps closed, or their blankets filled when Jim walked to the gambler's tent. He saw two kerosene lanterns burning outside the framed tent of H. William Lawton. The card man was still in business. Jim pushed back the flap and stepped inside. The tent was not tall enough to stand in, but there was a bench on one side of a solid looking table, and two chairs on the other. Three men sat at the table. Lawton looked up.

'Ah, Mr. Steel. I was hoping that you'd stop by. Care for a friendly little game?'

'How much would it cost me?'

Lawton laughed. 'That depends how well you play, how your luck runs, and how much you bet.'

'I've got a double-eagle.'

'That should get you at least a hand or two. We'll be done with this hand shortly.'

Jim sat and watched. They were playing draw poker, five cards, with jacks or better to open. The cards had just been dealt. He

78

watched the other two men, both miners. One he had seen before, a short man with a full beard and shiny black eyes. They were using paper money, gold dust and gold coins. The man with the beard had less than ten dollars left in front of him.

The second miner was young, maybe twenty, with sandy hair and shifting eyes. He had only four paper dollars in his table stake. The young man opened for a dollar. He discarded two cards. The bearded man sighed, threw away three cards and put his dollar in the pot. Both men had been pulling at pint bottles of whiskey at their elbows. Lawton was not drinking.

Lawton discarded two, put his dollar in the pot and lay down his hand. He dealt out the needed cards and slid his own together without looking at them.

'Bet a dollar,' the young man said.

The beard sighed, threw his cards face down on the pot and sighed again. Lawton met the bet and raised a dollar without looking at his hand. Sweat popped out on the young man's face. He had only two dollars left.

He took the two dollars and dropped them in the pot. 'Call,' he said, 'and raise you a dollar.'

Lawton watched him for a minute, and tossed in a dollar. 'Call.'

The youth gave a yelp of pleasure and laid down his hand. 'I outfoxed you that time, Lawton! Two pair queens over deuces!'

Lawton nodded. 'Good hand.' As the youth began reaching for the pot Lawton laid down his cards one pasteboard at a time. They came out a pair of jacks, an eight of spades, an ace of hearts, and the last card was a jack of hearts. 'Three jacks, looks like that means it's my pot,' Lawton said.

The youth with the two pair stared at Lawton for a long time, then got up barely able to control his anger. At the tent flap he turned and stared at the gambler. 'I wouldn't accuse a man cheating, Lawton, unless I could prove it and had my gun along. But I'll say you're good. That I will say.' He stormed through the flap.

Lawton laughed. 'The impatience of youth, especially when youth is also a loser on a not very good hand.' He waved Jim to a seat. 'Let me break up that double-eagle for you. Do you want paper money or gold?'

Jim said it didn't matter and the deck passed to the bearded miner, who said his name was Vance. He dealt with a slow deliberation, and because his hands hadn't recovered yet from the cold water. Chilblains were plaguing him and sometimes tears came to his eyes from the continuing pain in his feet and legs. He seemed to do everything slowly and with much thought.

'Five card stud,' the dealer said. It was a game that took the least thought and the fewest decisions. The ante was a dollar. The first card went face down on the rough hewn table that had been varnished until it was slick and clean. Jim's first face up card was a ten of spades, Lawton drew an ace of clubs and the dealer a seven of hearts. Lawton, being high with the ace, bet a dollar. All stayed in.

The second card around found Jim getting a jack of spades to go with the ten of spades; Lawton drew a five of diamonds not helping him with an ace and five; and the dealer doubling up with a pair of sevens. The dealer, Joey Vance, grinned.

'Goddamn, maybe my luck is changing! Glad you came on board, mate!' He bet two dollars as high hand and everyone was in.

The third round produced a queen of spades for Jim.

'Possible straight flush or a royal flush with his queen, jack and ten of spades,' Joe said with surprise. He laid down an ace of hearts for Lawton. 'The gambling man is high with a pair of aces and a five.' He dealt himself an eight of spades which didn't help his pair of sevens.

'Aces high,' the dealer said.

Lawton promptly bet three dollars for his pair and the dealer hesitated, then mumbling to himself, added two gold one-dollar pieces and a silver dollar to the pot.

The last round of cards produced no surprises. Jim got a second jack, ruining his royal flush chances. Lawton caught a five of clubs for two pair, aces and fives and setting him up for a possible full house depending on his hold card. The dealer pulled a seven of diamonds.

'Well, Goddamn, I'm high with three little sevens,' Joey said. 'I'm going the five dollar limit. Who's in?'

Jim looked at his hand. He had a face down card that showed a jack of hearts. He had anybody on the board beat. But did Joey hold another seven in the hole? It wasn't a good percentage bet to think so. Jim shrugged and put five silver dollars into the pot.

Lawton watched the little scene with pleasure. 'Now, the dealer hit something. His hand beats the table showing. But what's he got against my full house means I would carry the day. And our new friend, Mr. Steel, may have another jack hidden away. Possible. Or another queen, but that wouldn't beat the sevens and he's in, so he must have his jack. But I'm a gambler, so I'll bet my five and call you, Joe. What do you have?'

Joey grinned, his smile still in place. 'You can't bluff me, Lawton, you ain't got no full house. You see 'em. My three lucky sevens.'

Jim flipped over his hole card. 'Three jacks beats three sevens.'

Joey swore and they both looked at the gambler. Jim was sure Lawton had a full house, otherwise he would be beat on the board with the three sevens, and would have folded. To Jim's surprise the gambler shook his head, turned all of his cards face down and

82

pushed them to Jim as the next dealer.

'Beats me,' he said.

Jim frowned and watched him. No gambler would make a stupid five dollar mistake like that without a reason. But if he had a reason it wasn't a mistake. Was it a lead, a come-on, a con game? Jim pulled in the pot. It counted out to thirty-six dollars. He'd contributed twelve dollars himself, so he had just won twenty-four dollars, clean.

Joey stood up and swearing softly to himself, turned and walked through the tent flap without saying a word. The gambler lifted his brows and rubbed one hand over his face. He looked at Jim's face and saw the questions there.

'Why did I bet into a losing pot? Joey had lost too much tonight. I figured he had you beaten and I wanted to throw a fiver back his way. So I guessed wrong. That's a gambler's business, guessing. If I hit it every time, it wouldn't be gambling, would it?'

Jim picked up the cards and shuffled.

'But you knew I had Joey beaten or I wouldn't have bet in. You didn't want Joey to have the money, you're trying to con me. You must just have spent five dollars to soften me up.'

'Maybe, but you'll never know for sure, will you, Steel? Now, do you want to play some one-on-one?'

Jim paused, his eyes holding fast to those of

Lawton. At last he nodded. 'Why not. I came to lose twenty and so far I'm twenty-four ahead.'

They played. Halfway through the second game, Jim saw the dealer palm a card. It was neatly done, but not perfectly or Jim would never have seen it, Jim won the hand anyway to break even on the first two games.

When Jim dealt the fourth hand he shuffled the cards and adroitly left an ace on the bottom. He offered a cut of the deck to Lawton who shook his head. Jim dealt a game of five card draw with anything for openers. Jim held a pair of deuces in his hand and when the draw came he took three cards and gave Lawton the two he asked for. One of Jim's three came off the bottom, the other two off the top. Jim won the pot with the ace high over the deuces to beat Lawton's ace-king high.

Before the gambler started another hand Jim stood.

'I better be going. I have to work tomorrow.'

'You're leaving a winner.'

'So are you, a winner for the night's work. Thanks for the education.' Jim started for the door.

'I think it was you who educated me. That last game was a classic. You won it going away, and you didn't even need that ace.'

Jim stared at him sternly. 'Are you saying I cheated?'

The gambler chuckled. 'That is a word I

never use. Never. I'd rather say you are a man who has had a good deal to do with cards in his lifetime. I'd like to play you again, but for some reasonable stakes, that is if you'd care to gamble your skills against mine.'

'With an open call for counting the cards at any time?'

'Anytime,' the gambler said smiling.

'And a skin search?'

'Now that is going a bit far.'

'Then you won't mind if I furnish the cards?'

'Anytime.'

'Perhaps. But I'm sure a gravel washer like me wouldn't have nearly enough cash money to interest you, Mr. Lawton.'

'And I'm sure that you aren't just a plodding gravel splasher, Mr. Steel. I hope we meet again, soon.'

Jim walked slowly back to his camp thinking it through. Lawton was a gambler and he had seen him cheating. Ted McIntosh had played with him before his death. But would the man have a big winner killed just to get the money back? Or were they looking for something else? Some gamblers were cowards at heart and never even carried a gun. What about Lawton?

He thought about the other important items he had learned tonight. Ted had his rock hammer with him and he used it, evidently looking for the mother lode upstream. He may have deliberately stayed away from the heavy gold-bearing sand to help conceal the closeness of the lode. And Ted had said he'd need a lot of cash money. That must have meant he actually had found the lode and was getting together money and men to start his hard-rock claim.

Jim dropped beside the fire near where Lucas slept and stirred the embers. If the lode were there, he would find it. Somehow he'd figure a way to share it with Ted. That made him think of the family Bible he had taken from Ted's belongings. There might be a parent's name and address in it. He got the Bible and built up the fire so he could read the front pages.

There on the inside cover he found the family history with several neat, precise entries. It had been Ted's mother's Bible, showing her birthday and her wedding, then Ted's birth. A later entry showed Ted's father's death five years ago, and then his mother's death three years later. There was one entry after that.

It recorded the marriage of Ted McIntosh to Naomi Bunker on February 1, 1867, a little over six months ago. Jim closed the Bible and put it back with his things. Well, Naomi McIntosh, wherever you are, Jim thought. After he had the matters all settled here, he would find her. If there were a mine here, she would own half of it. If there were no mother lode, at least he could give her the thousand dollars in cash that Johnny Johnson was holding.

Jim made sure the fire was contained, then he went to move his horse and mule to a new picket area before he fell into his blankets and to sleep.

## CHAPTER SEVEN

## THE RED DEVIL'S ATTACK

Jim woke before dawn and already he could hear shouting, laughter and joking down by the general store. Almost everyone in camp would be there. It was a party, a roundup, a shivaree. The first store in Devil's Gulch was about to open. Jim got up and walked down to watch. Abe Lindstrom came to the door and sent two thundering blasts from his shotgun into the air to get everyone's attention. Half the camp's miners stood patiently in line.

'All right, you rat pack! Listen up. This is a store, not a Goddamn carnival. I let two men in at a time. When one goes out, another man gets inside. Don't try to steal nothing or you get shot with my .44 on the spot. No questions asked, you steal I shoot. Make sure to keep your hands in plain sight at all times, and don't push nothing down your shirt. In my store, my law is gut-shoot for stealing. So count that good. Gold dust and gold coin for payment, no damn paper! Okay, Bill, let the first two in.'

It wasn't that big an occasion for Jim so he went back to his camp, stirred up the fire and saw that Lucas was gone from his blankets. He must be in line to buy some food. Jim hustled up breakfast, some water-mixed flapjacks with sugar syrup. He had two pans of gravel washed before Lucas came back with a slab of bacon, a loaf of hard bread and two tins of sliced peaches.

'Thought I'd splurge a little,' Lucas said. He fried up six thick slices of the bacon and brought them to Jim between slabs of the fresh bread. It tasted better to Jim than a steak.

'Thanks, Lucas,' Jim said, an overtone of undisguised appreciation in his voice.

Lucas looked up and grinned. 'Hell, got to keep you healthy so you can show me where the rest of the gold is. I've seen you eyeing those outcroppings.'

'Is it that obvious?'

'Not to most of the men, but I watch you more'n most do. Oh, a few hard-rock men must wonder about the mother lode, but they ain't got the gumption to find it, let alone try to work it.'

'Well, I have,' Jim said.

'Yep, that's what I figured.'

Both laughed and Jim went back into the cold water and Lucas cleaned up his morning breakfast dishes.

Between pannings that morning, Jim made a better study of the bottom of the creek. Most of it was rocky with a few boulders but mostly small rocks, gravel, and sand. It made many places that slowed down the water to let the heavier gold particles drop out and collect. Jim looked across at the opposite bank where the first promising outcropping had showed. The free gold didn't come from that area, he was convinced now. The reason there was no gold dust just above him was that the bottom there was almost flat, some kind of sheet rock, so no gravel and little sand collected there.

Further up the bottom turned into a glassy, slick rock that channeled the water down a chute into the softer gravel bottom area where the water slowed and gold could fall. So the mother lode must be on above, and his lucky spot here was the first real place for the gold to collect.

At noon he took his sixgun and went hunting, rabbit-hunting he told Lucas, who only grinned. He wanted to explore upstream around the bend in the creek. A hundred yards from his claim he rounded the turn and was out of sight of most of the miners. Jim crossed the stream and checked the face of a cliff that the river must have cut its way through years and years ago. A nearly vertical wall rose twenty feet and almost from the water's edge. Jim could imagine this area during a spring runoff. It must surge with water a dozen feet deep.

Jim's practiced eye swept over the tops of the cliffs and for a moment he looked on, then he went back. He had seen something. Then he saw it again, the classic upthrust, the overlapped thrusting, the type of formation he had dreamed about so often and found so seldom. He stared at it again and tried to follow the course of the strata down through the cliff but couldn't. He went nearer the wall to check the face of the cut. Upstream fifty feet a huge piece of the rock wall had cracked and fallen away, leaving a square indentation a dozen feet deep and twenty feet high. Inside that void Jim studied the rock carefully.

He didn't believe it at first, then he checked again and he could see the faint traces of the quartz-beating gold ore that he had searched for so often. It was the raw edge of a vein of gold bearing quartz, and the river had been slicing away at it for centuries, sluicing away the gold, washing it free and depositing it along the stream bed.

He looked closer and then he saw a familiar sight—an area that had been chipped and gouged out with a rock hammer. He could see the imprint of the metal—he knew the signs. Someone had taken a sample and not more than a month ago. Ted McIntosh!

Jim's eyes widened for a moment. It was the starting place, the beginning. The mother lode might not be right here, but if this were one vein it could lead back to the larger vein and then perhaps to the mother lode.

Jim leaned against the rock, the ecstasy of

the moment surging through him, with the impact of a .44 slug. It was a feeling he would never forget. Jim blinked back the wetness and took a deep breath, then he went back to the stream and searched the wall further, but found nothing else to interest him. If anyone were watching him, he didn't want to seem overly interested in the rock wall. He shot as if trying for a rabbit, then turned back downstream. He was totally surprised no one else had found this wide open invitation to millions. But maybe it was as Lucas had said; nobody else here had the push to find and develop a hard-rock mine.

Jim panned the rest of the afternoon and at dusk went back to the face of the bluff. He was sure that Ted McIntosh had found the same spot. Before he got all the way to the strike, he saw four Ute Indians. They had not seen him; he stood quietly and let them pass on the other side of the stream. They were not hunting this time. They wore only loincloths and war paint, long yellow, red and white lines on their faces, chests and arms. Each brave carried a bundle of arrows and his bow. It was a war party. They moved silently toward the Devil's Gulch camp.

Jim faded higher into the brush away from the creek and ran hard for the tent site. He barely got there and passed the word that the hostiles were coming, when they heard a scream upstream. One of the miners on a claim just below Lucas's folded over and fell into the water, an arrow jutting from his back.

Jim threw two shots into the brush across the stream.

'Get down! Take cover!' he shouted. 'Get behind a log or a tree. Get out of the damn water! Indians, damnit, Indians attacking!' He fired four more times at a movement across the stream then reloaded as fast as he could. He had jumped behind a foot wide pine tree and stared past it. His head was a foot off the ground and he could see most of the stream. The last miner splashed out of the water and flopped behind a log and all was quiet for a moment.

One Indian showed upstream and drew two shots. It was almost as if he were attracting their attention. Jim turned and watched further below. He saw two Indians slipping downstream. Were they trying to get behind the miners? Jim slid from tree to tree shadowing the savages downstream until he came to the general store.

The miner above who had been hit in the back still floated in the water, face down. If the arrow hadn't killed him he was drowned by now.

Horses, Jim thought. The savages were after the horses. But all the animals were on this side of the creek, tethered or in a simple pole corral someone had built. It was a wait and see game for an hour, then the sun had dropped behind the ridge to the west.

Jim spotted one of the redskins sliding across the creek below the store. Jim waited until he was in range of the .44, then Jim leveled in and fired at the broad chest. His round caught the Indian just over the heart, slammed him backward and dropped him in the water. He never got up.

Two more Indians tried to cross the stream; Jim fired at one, hit him in the shoulder but he came on across, ducked in the first tent next to the general store, and a moment later backed out, an eight-inch Bowie knife jammed to the hilt in his stomach. He tottered toward the stream and two rifle slugs ripped into him, sprawling him backwards in death.

The other two Indians never tried to cross the stream. They retreated to the safety of the brush and began firing one arrow after another into the tents and the camp. Jim stayed behind a tree and waited. When the last arrow came in half a dozen men jumped up and splashed across the stream after the Indian.

'Come back!' Jim yelled at them. 'They aren't out of arrows, they'll pick you off one by one!' But the men wouldn't listen. 'Stay where you are for another ten minutes so we're sure they're gone,' Jim yelled. Most of the men did. When the time was up they scurried around trying to find out who was hurt. Two miners had been hit by arrows.

Johnny Johnson took an arrow in the right leg. The point passed through the fleshy part of his lower thigh and he broke the shaft off and pulled it out himself, then doused the wound with whiskey and tied it up with his shirt to stop the bleeding.

The second man, Ambrose, was dead. An arrow caught him in the throat as he leaned out from his pine tree trying to see the Indians who were shooting.

By then it was almost dark. The six men who had chased the Indians came back. They had been ambushed and fired upon and one man was dead, killed with an arrow through the heart. The men had emptied their guns into the brush and trees and carried their dead comrade home.

Jim pulled the dead man from the water and laid him beside the other two. The Indians were dumped in the common grave, and a foot of dirt spaded over them. The white men would have a decent Christian burial the next day.

Jim went to see the Miner's Committee chairman.

Stephano shook his head.

'We can't do it, Jim. Just who are we going to put on guard duty? We aren't trained Indian fighters. And who will give up a day of panning so he can protect the others who are panning gold?'

'All of these men have eyes,' Jim said. 'They all can see and listen and yell an alarm. Each man should have a gun near where he's panning, loaded and ready to fire. We can take

94

turns standing guards, or the guards can be paid an ounce of gold a day, with each miner putting some in a common treasury.'

Stephano stood and walked around his fire. 'Why did they attack? Who violated the sacred burial grounds? Will they be back?'

Jim stared at the Miner's Committee chairman. 'I don't think anyone violated the sacred grounds. Those four braves came looking for a fight. They had on war paint and a dozen arrows each. Those probably were the young bucks the chief said he might have trouble controlling. If so they will be punished for attacking without permission of their chief. Now is the time to show them that we are strong, that we will defend ourselves.'

Stephano lifted his hands in frustration. 'Jim, we don't even have a legal committee. We need another member. I'm appointing you to fill the third spot, and I won't let you say no and I don't want any complaints. We'll scratch up Win and do some business. Then you bring up the idea of your guards. I been around the Utes a bit. I'd say those young bucks had a belly full. Half their force dead, the other two out of arrows. My idea is they won't want any more of us all here.'

Jim thought over what Stephano had said. He had no real desire to be on the Miner's Committee, but if it would help smooth things down it might be worthwhile. The Utes were another matter. There would be some

95

retaliation by the braves, Jim was sure, but he didn't know when it would come. The two warriors would be back for vengeance if nothing else, with or without the chief's approval. Two warriors killed from a small band would be a serious loss. They would be back—he'd warn the miners to be alert.

'Stephano, I accept your appointment, but let's not meet right now. The camp is shook up enough with the attack. Let's let things simmer down for a while.'

'Good idea. See you in the morning, Jim.'

Jim walked back to his fire, telling the miners to watch out for Indians all the time, especially during the day.

Back at his own claim, he found Lucas working one last pan of gravel. His withered hand didn't hold him back much. He adapted to its limited function and took out almost as much gold dust as Jim could. Full darkness settled down quickly then and they built up the fire and got supper. It was the middle of September and the nights were getting colder at the high altitudes. Before long ice would be forming on the little puddles of still water during the night.

Jim leaned into the fire's heat and considered his two projects. If he didn't find the killer soon the camp might break up and then he'd never track down the person. On the other hand he had maybe two months before winter buried this whole valley under ten feet of snow. How could he start work on a mine then?

At least they were safe from the Indians now. Not even a Ute would attack at night; it was bad medicine. Jim took one more silent, furtive trip to his cache, added the new gold dust and came back as quiet as a moon shadow.

He had to find out how to stake out a hard rock mine. The rules changed from mining district to mining district. He could ask Stephano, he must have set up some kind of rules, dimensions, requirements. Tomorrow.

Together he and Lucas finished fixing their supper. Lucas put some potatoes and carrots and onions in the stew from the night before. He had kept it simmering all day so it wouldn't spoil. The night was cold enough to preserve it.

'I just keep throwing in new stuff all the time,' Lucas said. 'Once in Wyoming of a winter, I had one stew I ate for two weeks. Soon as I ate, I set the rest out and let it freeze. Then just put it on the fire for the next meal. 'Course after a while the meat kind of dissolves into the stew.'

Jim took his word for it and ate heartily, finishing the loaf of bread they had started that morning. The stew was delicious and a good change from the meager fare of the past few days.

The more Jim thought about his situation, the more he realized he was in the same trap that Ted McIntosh must have been in. He had his finger on the mother lode, but he needed

97

money to claim and start developing it. What should he do? If he went out of camp, back to Denver to raise the needed cash, somebody else might claim his gold mine. If he stayed here he didn't have the cash. The only answer seemed to be the same that Ted must have figured out. Try to raise the money right here in camp, play with the gambler for as much as he could get, then stake the claim and hire someone to maintain it and start to work. Then he could go into Denver when he had things underway and get the rest of the money he needed.

Lucas would be on his team, and he thought he could talk Johnny Johnson into working for him. He wasn't sure of anyone else. He would ask about hard rock men when the news got out, and there would be a handful interested. First he would have to open the face of the mine, start a tunnel, get some square-set shoring in and then build a road from the general store on up to the mine beside the creek. After that was done he could start bringing in equipment.

A stamping mill had to be one of the first projects, and they were not simple affairs. He had built one once before, powered it with steam. He was mentally placing the mill in the small valley, wondering about the tailings, how he could save the stream, what the river would do in the winter, and he worried about money, lots of money.

Jim kept thinking about his bank account in

Denver. What did he have there? Maybe fifteen thousand dollars? He'd need twice that to get the whole operation going. If it panned out. Maybe he should dig into the vein, and then take some samples in and have the ore evaluated, an assay. He could pile the ore in the open as he went. No one was going to steal it. Then if the vein developed and widened and did lead to the mother lode, he could use the assay with his bankers. The problem was right now he had only his reputation and his own $15,000 to borrow against. Even his own banker might not go along with that.

Lucas looked up from a smoldering corncob pipe. He had tobacco in it for the first time in three weeks. He blew a smoke ring and chuckled.

'Hey, Jim, you hear the talk?'

'What talk?'

'About Devil's Gulch? I saw three men packing up this afternoon. Before the Injun raid. First thing in the morning they're pulling out. The word is that Devil's Gulch is most panned out.'

'That so? I got almost three ounces today.'

'We're in the rich end. Most boys downstream are at less than half an ounce a day. At the price Abe is charging for food they say they can't even afford to eat, let alone buy equipment.'

'Figures to happen sooner or later. Getting colder too. Be freezing inside of two weeks.'

99

'Yep. So you better make your move soon.'

'Finding the killer?'

'Right, that too. What about the other?'

'I'm in the same trap Ted was. I need cash money. I need enough to get a toehold so I can get started, staked and legal, then hold it until I get to Denver for some real backing.'

'So?'

'So I need money.'

'I got maybe two thousand in dust, but that ain't big money.'

'It'll help, and I've got maybe three, and that other thousand of Ted's I'll invest. But we're still way short.'

'Only one man in camp will say ten thousand in dust.'

'The pasteboard man?'

'Right,' Lucas said.

'That's why I need a good night's sleep. I intend on paying a call on our gambling friend, Mr. H. William Lawton, first thing in the morning.'

'Is he the killer too?' Lucas asked.

'Could be. He's in it somewhere. We might just shoot rats with one four of a kind hand.'

'To do that you'd be pulling a few bottom cards, too,' Lucas said. He looked at the star-sprinkled sky. 'Lord help us all!'

# CHAPTER EIGHT

# HANGING TREE RENDEZVOUS

Jim woke before dawn, cold, cramped, miserable. He thought his nose was frostbitten. Jim kicked off the blanket and huddled around the coals in the carefully banked fire pit. Even the few glowing embers that remained seemed to be shivering. He decided the temperature was fifteen degrees colder this morning than it had been yesterday at the same time. Fall was here, winter was coming fast.

He fed small sticks into the coals until they blazed up, then added more wood and built it into a welcome, heat-producing fire. His hands slowly came back to life, and he rubbed his nose, then his ears and forehead. There was feeling after all.

Jim took his blanket, folded it and draped it over Lucas, who snored softly on his thin pallet near he fire. The sun wasn't up. Jim couldn't see the north star, so he dug out his round pocket watch and held it near the firelight on its rawhide thong to read it. The time was 4:32 A.M., much too early for man or beast, Jim thought as he put more wood on the fire, careful not to smother it so it had to use all of its heat to work on the new fuel. Jim nosed the blackened coffeepot onto the flat rock specially

101

positioned for that purpose and then reached for his canteen. The water in the canteen was frozen.

Jim found a pan and went to the creek, dipped out a quart of water and moved back to the fire. He saw half a dozen more campfires growing around camp. A lot of men were as cold as he was that morning. He found ice at the edge of the stream where the water lay still. They'd probably have it each morning now— until it really got cold. Jim made up his mind not to pan any gold today. He'd stay dry and a little warmer.

By the time Jim had the coffee boiled and settled down, Lucas kicked off the covers, noticed the extra blanket, and scowled.

'What's the matter, think I was gonna freeze to death?'

'Yes,' Jim said and handed him a tin cup of scalding coffee. 'Now get your toes up there to the fire before they drop off.'

They drank coffee, talked quietly and watched the dawn come. At last light tinged the eastern sky and later the first yellow rays hit the western ridgeline above them.

'Tarnation, Jim. How cold you figger it to be?'

'Twenty-eight, maybe twenty-nine. Water's gonna be colder than an old maid's bedroom.'

'I might take a short vacation,' Lucas said.

'You want to watch a poker game?'

'Not really,' Lucas looked up. 'You any

good cheating at poker?'

Jim laughed. 'I've been told so.'

Lucas grinned and went to get the bacon so he could slice the rest of it for breakfast.

The word darted around Devil's Gulch camp like a crazy lightning bug. Willy Walton had been murdered in his sleep, Johnny Johnson came up, hobbling on a makeshift crutch, his leg still hurting him where the arrow hit. He slid down beside the fire staring at the pan of frying bacon.

'You guys heard the news about Walton?' Johnny asked.

'Nope,' Lucas said. 'And you don't get no bacon.'

Johnson went on, ignoring the jibe. 'Walton went to the trouble of getting himself sliced up last night by a Bowie knife. One feller said Walton was stabbed ten, maybe fifteen times!'

'Robbed too?' Jim asked.

Johnson bobbed his head as Lucas filled a heavy cup with coffee and handed it to him. 'Yep. Him and his partner both, cleaned them out of dust. Most figure the robber was there and Walton woke up and met the end of that Bowie right through his heart. Walton was one of the ones moving out today.'

Lucas checked the pan-fried potatoes and onions, deemed them done and spooned them into three tin plates. He split the bacon three ways on the plates and handed Johnson a tin with a fork slanted into the food.

103

'Near as they can tell it was sometime after midnight. Walton went to bed late after he got all packed and ready. Even borrowed the gambler's lantern to finish his pack up and all.'

'He play cards much?' Jim asked.

Johnny chewed a big mouthful of potatoes and onions before he replied. 'He did some, yes he did use the cards now and then.'

Jim thought about it as he tended the fire. He finished his breakfast, picked up the axe, and went for some firewood. They needed some more of the heavy bark from the old conifer trees for cooking, and he wanted to find a stump he could kick apart and get out the sticks of pure sap deposits that burned like turpentine. With those dark brown deposits in the wood, you could start a fire in a blizzard. He kicked and chopped for half an hour. That gave him a chance to work off some frustrated energy and to think through a thing or two.

Back at the camp he put down the wood, sheathed the axe and told Lucas he was going to go talk to Stephano. The miner was out in the water already and told Jim to come back at noon. Winslow Carter would be there then too, and they'd have a regular mining committee meeting. Jim continued downstream to the store and wandered around inside. No one else was there and the owner, Abe Lindstrom, nodded when he came in.

'You're the new man made such a fuss at the Saturday night fire, right? Steel?'

104

Jim said he was.

'And you're the one Stephano wants to put on the miner's committee. Didn't ask me.'

'You're not a miner, Mr. Lindstrom.'

'Oh, yeah, true. Well, you're welcome to that committee. Two men been killed on it so far. I ain't about to get shot.'

Jim looked around the little store. It was dark, with only two small windows, a kerosene lantern burned in one end. There were two store-built tables, and two made of planks and log stubs. Merchandise hung from pegs on the walls, and in sacks and boxes. Jim found the potatoes, picked out a dozen, and took them up to the crude counter. There was no bar as in most mining camp stores. Abe was Mormon and wouldn't handle any sinful goods like whiskey or wine.

'Wrap up them taters good so they don't freeze.' Abe said. 'They go all black when they get froze.'

Jim paid a dollar for the twelve potatoes. Abe wrapped them up in an old newspaper and handed them to Jim.

Outside Jim sat on a stump and watched the little camp. It seemed to be on the wane, disintegrating. He saw only about half the staked claims were being worked that morning. Three more men had their horses next to their fires and were lashing on goods. Three more moving out.

Jim watched the two who had packed up the

105

previous night. They rode past him, turning down trail, with expectant grins on their faces, ready to find a new bonanza, to listen for the first rumor of strike anywhere in the west where they could ride, to try to get there first before the panning gave out. Jim waved at them and wished them luck.

He walked up to the other two men he had seen packing.

'Ain't no fit place for a body to live, no way, not in winter,' the first one said. He was in his thirties, raw-boned and whiskered, his face red from the cold. The other one admitted that he was scared. He was a small fat man, and wore a leather vest and mackinaw. 'I'm getting out while I can with what gold dust I got left,' he told Jim.

It was nearly ten that morning when Jim sauntered up to the gambler's tent. Lawton evidently had just got up. He was shaving at a crude stand outside his tent.

'Open for business?' Jim asked.

Lawton turned to see the speaker, then he smiled.

'Of course, Mr. Steel. I am always open and always at your service. Can you give me another minute to finish shaving?'

Jim nodded, sat on a log, and watched the men wading into the now nearly freezing water of the stream. He decided not to pan any more. Lucas could work his claim if he wanted to. He would sell it to Lucas.

The gambler finished shaving, slid the straight edged razor in its leather case and washed his face, then dried it carefully. A slap of bay rum on his face and he was ready. He slipped into a silk shirt and waved toward his tent.

'Shall we, Mr. Steel?'

Five minutes later the game was under way. Jim stared at the slightly smaller man for a moment, then took his sixgun out of its holster and laid it on the table near his right hand.

'Mr. Lawton, we both have played a lot of poker. I know, and you know, that no gambler can make a living for very long without employing certain questionable tactics—he cheats. Frankly, what I saw the last time we played led me to believe that you're not good enough at cheating to fool me. If I see you playing irregularly, you'll get a .44 slug through your right hand, and you'll never cheat at cards again. Do you understand completely my new house rules?'

'Absolutely, Mr. Steel.' Lawton took a .45 caliber Derringer from his pocket and laid it near his right hand. It had two barrels and at close range was as deadly as Jim's big .44. 'I also watched you cheating when we played, a useless dealing off the bottom. And I decided it was done carelessly so I would see and know that you were familiar with cards. If I see any of that type of play I will shoot you through the right elbow, and you'll never be able to do much of anything again.'

Jim nodded. 'Just so we understand each other. This is to be pure, honest poker, and let the luck fall where it may.'

They played for two hours. Only five-card draw poker was called, a high skill game where luck had the least margin. Lawton settled down and coolly played his game, taking the right cards, making the right bets. The cards fell his way and by noon Jim had lost a hundred dollars that he had brought with him, all in gold. On the last hand Lawton filled in a six of clubs for a full house and beat Jim's three nines. It was against all the odds.

'That's enough for today,' Jim said standing up. 'Maybe later tonight I might play again.' He smiled. 'Next time I'll bring more money.'

Lawton grinned, raking in the last pot, not really understanding. 'If you wanted to play for higher stakes, why didn't you bring your cash this morning?'

'I'm a night person,' Jim said. 'I think better, I play better, I have better luck, after dark. Shall we say ten o'clock?'

The gambler nodded and Jim walked out and uphill to his small camp where Lucas was busy cutting up a rabbit he had just skinned.

'That's where you been?' Lucas yelped when Jim told him he'd been playing cards. 'Land sakes. I'd have sent you out hunting if I'd knowed that. This here little varmint took me three shots. I guess I need practice.' He stirred the last of the cut up rabbit meat into the stew pot. 'The critter won't be done for an hour yet in case you was hungry.'

Jim said he'd be back and went to talk to Harry Stephano. The tall man came out of the water and walked to his fire, holding his hands out to the warmth.

'You ready to do business?' Jim asked.

Stephano said he was. He pointed to Winslow Carter who was walking up. The three men said hello and sat around Stephano's fire. The chairman took a small notebook out and the stub of a pencil, then wrote down the date, the place and the notice of a convened meeting.

*'Be it noted that on this date, September 15, 1867, a new member, Jim Steel, was appointed to this board and he accepted his duties.'*

'Is there any new business?'

'Yes,' Jim said. 'I move that the committee establish a wider range of crimes and punishments than we have now, to bring us more into line with the English Common Law practices. The first new law should be one dealing with robbery and theft. When such a crime is proved, it should be punishable by fines totalling all goods stolen, plus fifty percent of any goods that the convicted felon then owns, and his expulsion from the jurisdiction.'

The other two men looked at Jim. Winslow nodded.

'Fine by me,' Winslow said.

'All in favor,' Stephano said and the motion carried three to nothing.

'Do we have any procedures for filing other than placer claims?' Jim asked.

'No,' Winslow Carter said.

'Why don't we simply establish that the rules and regulations governing hard rock claims shall be the same as those of the federal mining laws? That way we're covered if we need to be.'

Winslow nodded. 'Told Stephano weeks ago we should have that on our books, just in case. I so move.'

They passed it unanimously, then Stephano appointed Jim to bring in a minimum set of coded laws to move them closer to a civilized community, and the session broke up.

Winslow Carter walked along with Jim to the river.

'You hear anything about a hard-rock strike?' Carter said.

'Fact is, I haven't heard a word. Are you a hard-rock man?'

Winslow stopped and scratched his head, then put his hat back on. 'Used to be, over in Nevada. Did a little silver. But every man here knows this color has to come from somewhere. I guess nobody's got the gumption to find out where.' He pointed up stream. 'Two more men leaving. Devil's Gulch is dying. Now we have more men leaving than coming in. Getting too damn cold. This place will be a one-cabin no-tent town in another month.'

'You may be right. What about the killing? Shouldn't we do something about that?'

'Not unless we have a suspect and some witnesses. We can't act as a police force too. If some citizen complains, and gives us a suspect and swears as a witness, then we have a trial.'

'So, without a sheriff, without a district attorney...'

'Right. It's primitive, but it's all we can afford, and it works to a certain degree.'

They parted and Jim watched the camp. He could see that the first signs of decay had started. Two men leaving each day wouldn't take long to clean out the whole camp. He'd seen it happen before. Soon they'd be going in threes and fours, then half a dozen. He walked back hoping the rabbit was cooked.

Just as he came around the brush this side of their camp, Jim saw two men with Lucas. One held the old man and the other punched him in the stomach. Jim drew and fired one round into the air as he crashed across the trail into the camp and slammed his fist into the first man's jaw, spinning him backwards. The second man let go of Lucas and tried to get away, but Jim nailed him with a running tackle and rolled over once on the ground, then smashed his fist into the man's jaw and sat on top of him. The first man jumped to his feet and ran away downstream.

Lucas came up and kicked the man on the ground in the side.

'Dirty sidewinder! Caught them trying to steal my rabbit stew. The ornery skunks. Told them to go shoot their own varmint.'

Jim let the man up and asked him what he was doing beating up on an old man.

'Hell, we was just hungry. Used up our dust on food and it's all gone. Panning ain't no good down there.'

'Then ride out,' Jim said. 'If you can't hack it, ride on. You want a broken arm as a reminder?'

The man with the small mustache and red vest shook his head and edged backward. 'No, sir. No, sir. I sure don't. Didn't mean no real harm.'

Jim caught him by one arm and ran him to the creek, tripped him and pushed him into the ice-cold stream with a water-churning splash.

'You better ride out of here, pardner,' Jim said. 'I don't want to see your face around Devil's Gulch again.'

The rabbit was cooked to a turn, and with some salt it was the best Jim had tasted in years.

Lucas looked little worse for the fight. Jim had arrived after the second punch, but Lucas swore he'd have sore ribs for weeks.

Right after the noon meal, Lucas took out

his sixgun and a box of .44 shells and began shooting. 'I figure the better shot I am with this thing, the safer. Shore wish I'd been wearing it this morning. Then those hog-tailed varmints never would have treed me.'

He kept blasting away at a bush across the creek, then at a tin can, until the box of rounds was gone. A few miners came up, watched a minute, then retreated.

'I can knock the legs off a horsefly at fifty feet,' Lucas told them. 'This morning I got sloppy and hit the fly in the head, so I got to do a mite of sharpening up.'

That afternoon Jim cut four new corner stakes, poles five feet long and five inches in diameter. He squared off the tops of each one, then skinned the bark on top and flattened a side so he could print on the wood, then sharpened the end of each of the stakes. He and Lucas went together to stake out the new hard-rock mine. Federal regulations called for a hard rock claim to be six hundred feet wide and fifteen hundred feet long. He used the six hundred feet along the face of the cliff and extended it down to the old line of his panning claim. The fifteen hundred feet came four hundred feet on the camp side of the river, and the other eleven hundred across the river and up the slope of the wider side of the small valley to clear enough space for a stamping mill. Maybe a bunkhouse and a cook shack could go downstream. He would also need a cabin, an office and a storage shed or two to keep things out of the snow. He might not get it all done in the next two months. Jim scowled. There was absolutely no chance he would get it all done before snow time.

When he had his stakes pounded into the ground, he walked down to Stephano's and told him he wanted to file on a new claim.

'You giving up on your rich one?' the Mining Committee chairman asked.

'Nope.'

'You can only file on one claim at a time in this district.'

'That's all I'm filing on. This one includes my former claim.'

'Hard rock claim?'

'Yes.'

Stephano gave the book to Jim where he wrote in the location of his new claim and specified that it was six hundred feet by fifteen hundred feet and infringed on no other claim, territory or owned property.

Stephano's eyes narrowed. 'So you had the mother lode spotted all along.'

'Not for sure, but I'm willing to take a shot at it. It sat there waiting for any of you to go get it, but the only man who tried must have been Ted McIntosh, and he got killed doing it.'

'I guess most of us wouldn't know what to look for. Oh, it's yours, all legal. Only trouble is, winter's coming, and to prove up on a claim you have to be on it every five days.'

114

'I know, that's why I want to get as much done as I can before the snow starts. You want to stay and work?'

Stephano shook his head. 'No, I like to work for myself. I'm going to Arizona for the winter. My blood is getting too thin to stay up here in snow time.'

Jim headed back toward his fire, and the news of a hard rock claim moved faster than he did; it was like a forest fire. By the time Jim got back to his camp, there were two men there and a dozen came running up.

'Hey, Jim, you need some men?'

'How much you paying?'

'You give board and room?'

'When can we go to work?'

Jim waited for the talk to die down, then he told them that he would be needing a dozen men to start. He was paying regular mining wages.

'It's eight dollars a week topside, and ten dollars in the tunnels and shafts. We don't give board and room, but we'll try to get up winter quarters as soon as we can. You'll have to work at cabin-building too until we get moving.'

Jim had them give their names and experience to Lucas who produced a pencil and notebook and began writing down the details. When the last man left, Jim took the notebook and leafed through it. Some of the men had gold mine experience, or so they claimed. Others silver mining. A few said no experience.

115

A new face edged toward the fire, it was that of the dwarf. Mars Duncann scowled and handed Jim a piece of paper. The dwarf waddled back out of the way as Jim read the message.

*Mr. Steel. I understand that you want to know more about how Ted McIntosh died. I know. I can tell you. Meet me at the hanging-tree at midnight. Come alone, or I won't be there. If you will come, tear this note in two and give half to the little man. Mars is safe, he can't read, write or speak.*

The note had no signature. Jim promptly tore the paper in half and handed one part to the dwarf, who took it and scampered off downtrail.

Jim watched him go. He could follow the little man, but if he did the man who wrote the note would not show himself. Whoever gave Mars the note would get the answer eventually. Jim knew he would have to go tonight to discover who wrote the note and then try to dig more information out of him. It might be some help, and again, it might not be. But Jim knew he would go; he couldn't pass up such a good chance.

## CHAPTER NINE

# THE MIDNIGHT SHOOTOUT

Jim didn't play poker that night. He cleaned and oiled his new rifle. It was a used weapon in excellent condition that he had picked up in Denver, a Ballard single shot cartridge rifle. It was made in 1865 and just missed action in the civil war.

The Ballard was an authority whenever it spoke with its .56 caliber size, and could knock a man a dozen feet backward when the big slug made contact. The barrel was thirty inches long, and perfectly round as contrasted with the octagonal barrels of many long guns. Total length was forty-five inches, which made it awkward to carry on a horse, but Jim was partial to it right now. It had a leaf rear sight graduated up to five hundred yards.

The operation was simpler than some others in use. With the Ballard you swung the trigger guard extension down and forward which dropped the breech mechanism, exposed the chamber for loading, and brought the hammer to half-cock safety. Extraction of the used shell was manually operated by sliding a stud under the barrel which was drawn rearward pulling the cartridge out of the chamber. Jim had paid thirty dollars for the rifle and two hundred rounds.

Lucas was still against Jim's going to the hanging tree.

'You can't tell who might be hiding in the brush up there,' Lucas said. 'Why they could have five or six guns just waiting for you.'

'True,' Jim said. He polished the stock of the Ballard and put some more wood on the fire. 'But if all they want is me dead, they have a good chance every night. A man sitting next to a blazing fire in the dark makes a perfect target. But nobody's tried for me here yet, except for that one time.'

'Then I better go along,' Lucas said.

'Not a chance. The note said to come alone. Besides, I'm going to get up there long before anyone has a chance to get into an ambush position. I might even have some surprises for them. Oh, I need to borrow your sixgun for a while.'

'You got two, why you want another one?'

'A surprise for my guests.'

Lucas gave it to him, then rummaged in his carpet bag and came up with a second revolver. 'I better get this one into working order.'

Jim left the campfire as soon as it was fully dark. He took his rifle and the three sixguns and went downstream, just past the cliffs, forded the river on a scattering of dry rocks, and vanished silently into the brush that circled the small open place on the little shelf where the hanging tree stood. The growth came within

118

fifteen feet on one side, and that's where Jim headed, moving without sound through the brush, his senses alert for any smell or movement which might betray an ambusher. He searched each area carefully before moving ahead and soon decided that he was alone.

Jim took a ball of strong string from his pocket and figured out his lines of fire. Then he tied his own sixshooter to a tree with a length of rawhide, fixed it tightly so it wouldn't wiggle, and tied a special loop of string around the inside of the trigger and the back of the trigger housing. He cocked the weapon and played out the string. It would be a one shot surprise, but that should be enough. He didn't want to kill anybody, just capture one and make him talk. It shouldn't be too hard.

Jim went ten yards away and found an opening in the brush where he rigged the second revolver the same way, aiming it at the hanging-tree. The string from that one trailed back through the undergrowth to where the other string lay.

Next, Jim moved silently to the hanging-tree. He arranged a blanket and his spare jacket against the trunk of the pine and placed his low crowned gray hat on top. It looked as if Jim Steel was slumped down waiting for a meeting.

Jim returned to his ambush spot. He was positioned on the far side of the clearing from the camp, and he guessed the attackers would set up close to him before they discovered the dummy at the tree. Jim checked his lines of fire, then settled down behind a small blind of branches he had built, and waited.

The cold bored into him. He had on his sheepskin coat and a heavy stocking cap, but still the cold drove into every bit of exposed flesh. His ears tingled. He had at least two more hours to wait. Jim hadn't figured out his exact play. Should he capture the first person who showed up, or wait and see if they were laying a trap, hoping to kill him quickly before fading back into camp? He would play it by ear, do whatever seemed best at the moment.

He waited.

An hour later Jim had identified three night birds, and had seen rather than heard a large owl fly past, its wings cutting the air in silent flight to enable it to slip up on night feeding mice, rats and even rabbits. The moon came out, the night air snapped crisply and the stars at this altitude hung so close to the treetops Jim thought he could stretch up just a little and catch one.

He buried his gloved hands deep in his armpits to help keep his fingers from tingling. It was below freezing already, he guessed, and would be colder before morning. Winter was coming too fast, and he had too much work to do.

Jim checked his railroad pocket watch and was just able to see in the moonlight the time on the large figured face. It was eleven o'clock.

He heard the first movement long before he saw anyone. A branch broke campward. Then he heard footsteps coming quickly, with little thought of concealment or silence. A shadow pushed out from an overhanging pine at the edge of the clearing. It was a full-sized man, not a dwarf, but Jim couldn't recognize him. He was about fifty feet away. The man looked at the hanging-tree and then settled into a small clump of brush near a small pine. Jim studied the area closely until he knew he could find the exact spot where the man vanished. Then he picked up the two strings and tested them. Each one had a straight pull from him to the gun. Jim decided to wait.

Two minutes later he heard a night hawk call. There had been no night hawks in this area before. Indians? He didn't think so. To his right the call came again. He saw the shadow in front of him move slightly, then give the worst imitation of a hawk call Jim had ever heard. There were two of them so far.

Jim never saw the second man. He stayed deeper in the brush but he was to the left, the other man to his right, and both in front, between Jim and the camp.

Another ten minutes oozed by, slowly, deliberately. Then Jim heard something at the far end of the clearing. A moment later a horse broke through a screen of brush and rode hard for the hanging-tree. The rider wore all black.

Jim thought the man had on a kerchief mask but he wasn't sure. He rode to the tree, saw the form in the shadows and fired four shots into the blanket, then wheeled his horse. As he did Jim leveled in with the Ballard and squeezed off a round at the men's torso. The heavy Ballard thundered into the silent night air and Jim saw the man spill off the horse. Jim pulled one of the strings and a sixgun went off to his left. He reloaded the Ballard quickly and sighted the first man in the brush across from him. He fired once with the Ballard, then pulled the last string and the second sixgun went off, belching a flamed blast in the darkness and sending its lead messenger slamming toward the hanging-tree.

Jim looked at the horse and rider. The rider lay on the ground near the tree. The horse had pranced away a few feet and now stood, head down nibbling the frosty glass. Nothing else moved. Jim heard hurried footsteps crashing through brush as someone ran back to camp. No other sound came.

Jim ran low and silently toward the hanging-tree, though the brush, then, at the last moment, into the open. He put the tree between himself and the gunman on the ground. He made it to the rough bark of the big pine without taking rounds. Jim peered around the tree at waist level. His coat was still there, his hat had fallen to one side. Six feet in front of the dummy lay the form of the rider. His hands were in plain sight, and carried no weapon. Jim rushed to him and pulled down the mask. He had seen the miner before, but he didn't know his name. The heavy .56 caliber bullet had ripped through the man's chest, came out his back, and almost tore his jacket from his shoulders.

Jim ran low, his .44 ready in his hand as he headed for the second gunman in the shadows. Before he got there Jim heard a low moan, and he stopped, then moved more cautiously. The last dozen feet he went in a rush, the .44 in front of him, the sights dead center on the man's shadowy chest. The enemy's hands made no move, his head came up slowly.

'God but it hurts!' the bearded man said.

Jim frowned and then started with surprise at the face of Winslow Carter, the third man on the Devil's Gulch Miner's Committee.

'Carter, you?'

Winslow Carter looked, a snarl of his face now. 'Me, damn right me. I only pulled in a quarter of an ounce today. I need to make money like everybody else.'

'But an ambush, a bushwhacking, murder? You helped try to kill me!'

'No such thing. I'm just a guard. If anyone tried to come down this way I was to fire over his head.'

'And what about the joker on the horse who pumped five slugs into the dummy up there he thought was me?'

'They didn't tell me it was a killing. I didn't know anything about that.' He groaned again. 'Can you stop the bleeding?'

Jim looked at Carter's thigh. The slug had torn into it high, angled down and came out the back leaving a large hole. Blood flowed freely.

'I *could* stop it and save your miserable life.'

'If I tell you what?'

'Who hired you to kill me.'

'The jasper on the horse, the one you killed. He's the only one I saw. He gave me ten dollars gold to sit here and wait.'

Jim believed him. 'Looks like you waited a little too long, Carter.'

'Are you going to stop the bleeding?'

'I'm trying to figure if you're worth saving. I could just walk away.'

'God, Jim! Don't do that. I didn't know who they were after. So help me, they didn't say. Just to sit here and guard this area, that's all they told me. If they said it was you, I'd have come and warned you. Honest!' There was a desperation in his voice, and appeal for life that Jim couldn't deny. He tore off a piece of Carter's shirt, made two compresses of it and used a bandage to tie them in place. By then the pain was boiling through Carter.

'Can you walk with a crutch?' Jim asked.

Carter started to say he could, then he passed out. Jim put his rifle against a small tree and picked up Carter. He used the fireman's carry, looping Carter's arm across his neck, hoisting the man on his shoulder, then grabbing his good leg.

Jim worked his way back to camp, down the slope, across the gurgling creek, and into camp. Everyone there seemed to be sleeping. Not even the boom of the heavy rifle had roused the tired miners.

Jim found Carter's camp and laid him down on his blankets. He built up the fire and examined the wounds again, doused them with whiskey and then rebandaged both areas. This time he tied new compresses in place, made from the ripped sleeves of a shirt. Then he built up the fire and roused Carter's friend to keep the blankets on the unconscious man and to feed the fire so Carter didn't freeze to death. Jim didn't say what happened to Carter and the cooking mate didn't ask. He was a small man with a full beard and his eyes were frightened.

Before Jim left he said that Carter had been shot in the leg and he'd need some tending to the next few days. Then Jim went back to the hanging-tree, picked up his rifle, the two sixguns, his jacket and hat, and took one more look at the body. Time enough in the morning to figure out what to do about it. Carter was his only witness and he might not want to talk. Jim picked up his blanket and hat and trudged back to camp. He was tired, but at least he was alive—that was saying a lot this day.

Back in his camp, Jim rolled into his

blankets, but couldn't sleep. It was almost 2:00 A.M. before he dozed off, and he had a feeling the night had warmed up instead of getting colder. The only thing he could think of was that he had killed the man he needed to question, the man who knew the connection. It all had to lead back to the man who had killed Ted McIntosh. The same man must have tried to bushwhack him.

The new mine was common knowledge now. Anybody could have engineered the attack. But who would have ready money to make the payoffs? He should have checked the horseman's body, it might have had some clues.

But right then, in Jim's sleep-fogged mind, he could think of only two men in camp with any amount of cash money ... no three: Johnny Johnson, the merchant, Abe Lindstrom, and the gambler. Yes, the gambler. He needed to sit down with the man and reason him out of some poker winnings.

\*     \*     \*

When Jim woke again it was warmer. No ice, no frost, clear and cold, but with air twenty degrees warmer than the previous morning. He had breakfast ready by daylight and Lucas came up yawning and sniffing the bacon, flapjacks, and coffee. The bacon was from a fresh slab Jim had bought from the storeman the day before.

'See you're still here,' Lucas growled waking up slowly.

'Just barely,' Jim said and told Lucas the story.

'Don't go to no more night meetings,' Lucas said.

'I won't. Today we get the mine started. You ever put up a log house?'

'One or two,' Lucas said dryly.

'Good. Pick out a spot in the farthest downstream corner of our claim and clear it for a ten-by-twenty-foot cabin. Hire two or three men. Then go see Johnny Johnson and tell him we need that paper money he's holding, that thousand. We can use it for operating capital until I clear out the gambling man of his ill-gotten gains.'

Lucas looked up. 'You trying to bribe me with bacon and flapjacks and coffee, son?'

Jim laughed. Nobody had called him 'son' in a long time.

'No, grumpy, I'm not. I'm just trying to figure out how to hire you the cheapest way. Wondering whether you'll want to take a short view and work for twenty dollars a week, or whether you'll take a ten percent partnership in the Devil's Gulch Bonanza gold mine.'

Lucas dropped his fork. 'A ten percent partnership? You really mean that?'

'Yes, Lucas. You've earned it. And you'll go right on earning it. How about it?'

'Judas Priest! How do I get myself in these messes? I don't want no responsibility.'

'Lucas, I'd say you're a man who has shouldered responsibility most of his life, a man who is a little lost without it, and who can help me one hell of a lot in the next three months before we get snowed in. I'd like to make it a bigger share, but fifty percent of this claim is going to be in the name of Naomi McIntosh, Ted's widow. I found her name in that family Bible.'

'That leaves you only forty percent...'

'More than I need. Now are you with me?'

A tear seeped from the old man's eye and he brushed it away quickly. Another took its place. For the first time in many years Lucas Brace felt so much emotion swelling up in his throat and chest that he couldn't talk. All he could manage was a nod.

Jim patted his shoulder. 'Good, Lucas, I'm glad you're with me. I feel a lot better now. I'm going to look at the face of that cliff again and decide where we start the first tunnel. We'll want to put the stamping mill as close by as we can so we have the shortest haul of the ore. You might want to buy a couple more axes from anybody who's leaving camp. We'll be needing them. Pick out two or three men you want and get moving on that cabin. Otherwise we'll all be freezing our asses in a snowbank come December.'

Lucas dabbed at his eyes, tossed the dirty

dishes in a stack and strapped on his sixgun. He nodded at Jim again, took his notebook and headed downstream to catch the men he wanted before they got their feet wet in the cold water.

The next thing Jim did was reload his sixguns, put one away and take the other and an axe as he went toward the hanging-tree. He might as well be the one to find the body as anyone.

As he came to the clearing he saw that the horse was not there. It probably wandered away in the night, or perhaps was grazing, he decided. He walked through the fringes of brush into the open and on toward the hanging-tree.

Jim stared in surprise at the emptiness around the big tree. The body was gone. There was no evidence at all that a man had died there last night. Jim moved to the exact spot where the body had been and found only one small stain of blood in the hard earth. Someone had cleaned up the evidence, even the horse.

Jim looked at the base of the pine and saw where two of the slugs from the dead man's .44 had blasted through his hat and into the tree. Jim continued walking through the cleared area and in the woods, then swung back toward his claim.

Someone not only wanted him dead, but went to a lot of trouble to try to kill him. Then when it backfired he removed the evidence, now there was no way to trace the man behind it. It worried him. Every day that passed would make it harder and harder to find the man or men who killed Ted McIntosh.

But he had to get the mine started, or winter would smother them. First things first.

Jim spent all morning looking over the land he had claimed. He had a mental picture of the terrain, where it sloped off, where the levelest spot was he could use high against the side of the ravine for his stamping mill. He was right, he'd have to use steam power, the force of the water in the little stream wasn't strong enough to turn a paddle wheel that would provide enough power.

When he had the entire area clear in his head, he went back to camp and put it down on paper. He'd go back later and mark off the distances by paces, but so far it looked practical. The stamping mill would be almost directly across from tunnel number one. They would make some kind of a bridge for the ore carts to go across the stream. It would have to be strong enough so it wouldn't wash out in the spring runoff.

Jim went deep into his paper plan when he heard the first yell from downstream. Then there were shouts, cheers, and screams. He heard a few gunshots, and thought little of it. Then a particular scream came through and jolted him. It sounded like a woman!

He jumped up and heard three quick shots,

the universal signal for help. Jim touched his sixgun to be sure it was there, and left his fire on the run pounding down the trail toward the sounds. They increased. Others were running as well. Now he saw a few men coming back the other way loaded with sacks and packages and boxes. Jim asked them what was happening, but no one replied.

He charged the last few yards and saw a team and a wagon stopped near the log-cabin store. The cover had been torn off it and half the goods were scattered on the ground or already stolen. Six men pawed through the boxes on the wagon. From somewhere came the groaning scream of a woman.

Jim fired once into the air, then he shot the man on top of the wagon through the leg, slamming him backwards to the ground. A shot came from the other side and another voice, Jim knew to be Stephano boomed through the quiet air.

'Get off there, you thieves, we'll have no looting here.'

Jim put another bullet into the air and the last man scrambled down from the wagon. Jim drew down on a man dragging a sack, blasted a round under his feet, until he dropped the sack and ran.

Jim rushed to the wagon and found it to be a total disaster. Flour sacks were broken open. A hundred-pound sugar sack ruptured, canned goods scattered.

Lucas came in from the other side with Stephano, both with smoking guns at the ready. They saw Jim and relaxed.

Jim saw a hand stretched up from a pile of boxes. Carefully the three of them lifted the goods away until they found a small Chinese man with a long pigtail.

He sat on the ground, bleeding from his nose and mouth, a huge bruise growing on his forehead. He bowed where he sat and Jim bowed back. Then the little man used what few English words he knew.

'Wife? Where Chow Ling wife?'

## CHAPTER TEN

## YOUR SLAVE FOR LIFE

'Your wife?' Jim asked. 'A woman came here with you? On the wagon?'

The dazed Chinese man nodded, then began jabbering in Chinese.

A scream came then, muted, strangled, but loud enough so they could hear it and tell from what direction it came. Jim led the charge into the brush beside the cabin. One man sat at a woman's head, his hands around her throat strangling her. Another man knelt between her parted legs, her skirts were bounded around her waist and he had mounted her.

Jim shot the man kneeling first, the .44 slug slamming cleanly into the side of his head, blasting him off the woman, rolling him to one side. The man choking the woman jumped up in terror and panic, his right hand digging for a holstered gun. Jim let him get it out, then shot the man once through the heart. He lunged backward then lay still.

The Chinese man ran forward, fell on his knees beside his wife and stared at her. She hadn't moved. He bent and listened to her heart, examined the long white marks on her throat, then folded her hands on her chest, smoothed down her skirt and sat back on his heels facing her. He bowed three times, so low his head touched the ground. The chanting song that came from his mouth was different from anything Jim had ever heard.

The chant must have had its roots in the agony of the first man when he lost a loved one, as he tried to vent his pain and frustration, his anger at unknown gods, his sorrow, his fear. The waiting chant soared and cried, it jolted downward, then came up again in a series of softly painful passages, punctuated with gutteral and angry parts. It seemed to finish, then it came again.

Lucas, Jim and Stephano went back toward the wagon.

'He'll be there at least an hour,' Lucas said. 'I saw lots of Chinese in San Francisco.' Lucas waved his .44 at a would be looter and he ran back up river. Abe Lindstrom came to the door of his store and surveyed the damage, shook his head and went back inside.

Jim recruited six men who were standing around watching, and ordered them to clean up the mess of the wagon, to salvage what they could of the flour and sugar, and to put everything back on the wagon. When it was ready, Jim drove the rig as far up the creek bank as it would go. With a lot of effort the team dragged the wagon to Jim's claim, and there he unhitched the horses.

Jim left Lucas as guard and went back to talk to Harry Stephano.

'We've lost our hold on the men,' Harry said, sitting beside his fire, looking now and then at the brush where the Chinese still sang his death song.

'Not necessarily,' Jim said. 'We can get it back tonight with a campfire and have every man there. We'll simply tell them we have a strong set of laws and there will be no more robbing, looting or killing.'

Harry looked up, disbelief in his eyes. 'But you killed two men this afternoon. How can you explain that?'

'Rape is against our law. The two men were attempting to rape the Chinese lady and in so doing murdered the victim. I was acting as an officer of the court, a member of the Miner's Committee, and as the duly appointed law officer and sheriff named by the Committee yesterday.'

Stephano held his head and stared into the fire. 'It's probably just as well this happened. I should be moving on. I don't think the men will accept your answers. You've come in here like a cyclone. Some of the men don't like you.'

'It doesn't matter if they like me, as long as they obey the laws. Some of them don't like me because I found the mother lode they were too lazy to look for. Now with the mine going in we need law and order more than ever.'

'I don't know, Jim. Maybe I'm getting tired, too old. I've tried so hard to make this thing work, to make a stable society.'

'And you've done a good job. This camp is ten miles as safe as some I've been in. Now it's time for us to take another step, to move on. To develop into a more stable society, led by the men who want to settle down and stay here.'

'I don't know,' Stephano said. 'It's so hard.'

'Anything worthwhile is hard, Harry. At least we can try it. What have you to lose? You're still panning, and if you don't want to pan anymore, I'll hire you at the mine.'

Harry looked at him, put another stick on the fire and then stood up. 'You're right, Jim. Let's try it. I hate to leave a job half finished. I'll start spreading the word about a campfire tonight, about a Committee report and that everyone should be there.'

'Good, now you're thinking right. Will you take care of the two dead men, too?'

Stephano sighed, and nodded. 'Yes, and I'll watch the Chinaman, Chow Ling. He'll want to have some type of burial for his wife. He didn't look badly injured to me.'

'Just punched around a little. Tell Chow Ling we have his wagon up at the last claim with most of his goods. It's all his and we'll help him protect it until he decides what he wants to do.'

That night the Committee campfire meeting went about the way Jim expected it would. The owners of the better placed claims were enthusiastic, said they were ready to pan until there wasn't any gold left, then they could start work at the mine. Twenty-six men came out for the meeting. Four others said they were leaving the next morning. The gambler even attended since he had no other business. He watched, but couldn't vote.

A show of hands was used as a vote of confidence that made Jim the official law officer of the district. Of the twenty-six miners there, at least half indicated they would stay and work in the mine after the panning petered out.

Stephano closed the meeting on a solid note.

'Gentlemen, we are a self-governing group of men. We are a true republic where we all vote on everything. We elect our leaders, our lawman, we make our laws. That means we take care of ourselves, we watch out for neighbor, we respect the rights of each individual. And we care about each other. This has to be a happy, concerned family of men here. If we can't learn to get along peacefully and happily, then we'll all wind up in unmarked graves. We can't have any more looting, murdering, or stealing in our little community. Most of the bad apples are gone. If you know of any more in our small barrel, we must get rid of them at once. This we can do with a two-thirds majority expulsion order. This simply forbids the person from living or working in our district. What I'm saying is let's be friends, true and honest friends. Let's learn to live together and work together, and then let's all hope that we can get rich!'

When the meeting was over, Lucas and Jim went out to the corner of their claim against the edge of dark hill. They were only a hundred and fifty feet from the little stream, but it was as far toward the hill as they could push. Even so it would take two or three feet of excavation to get the land flat enough to build the cabin. Lucas and his men had cut down six trees from the cabin spot and cleared off half of the brush.

'A fine day's work,' Jim said. 'Hire two more men tomorrow. I can already feel that snow coming.'

Back at the fire, Jim dug into a seam along the bottom of one of his jackets and took out a hundred dollar bill.

'For emergencies,' Jim said as he showed it to Lucas. 'Right now I'm in need of more

137

payroll money, so I'm going to the bank to make a withdrawal.'

'We got a bank here?'

'Sure. The H. William Lawton Bank and Gambling Emporium.'

Jim found the lanterns lit outside Lawton's tent, an invitation that the gambling game was still open. Jim edged through the tent flap just as the dwarf came out. He scowled at Jim and faded into the darkness.

Jim looked at Lawton who had three men at his table.

'I didn't know Mr. Duncann worked for you, Mr. Lawton.'

The gambler looked up, pleased to see new money walk in. 'He doesn't, he just lost twenty dollars and I'm always friendly to a man of any stature who wants to lose money at my table.'

'What about a man by the name of Ted McIntosh, did he ever play here?'

Lawton returned Jim's stare evenly. He never twitched a muscle or showed any surprise. 'I don't recall the name, Mr. Steel. But if he panned for gold in Devil's Gulch, then he probably came to my table at least once before he moved on.'

'I didn't say he had moved on. Fact is he was killed right here.'

'Right here, Mr. Steel?'

'Right in this camp. Then his body was stuffed under a lightweight sluice box that wouldn't drown one of your dwarfs, and the verdict came as accidental drowning. It was no drowning, he was murdered.'

'A friend of yours, Mr. Steel?'

'Damn right, a good friend. And I'm here to even the score with Ted's killer.'

'But in the meantime, how about some poker? Or did you come here just to talk?'

'You have an open chair?'

'We do, and it's yours.'

Jim sat down and watched the end of the game of seven card stud. The dealer lost, Lawton won. One of the miners left the game. Jim produced his hundred dollar bill and the three men looked at it closely.

'We don't see many of those out here,' Lawton said. He deftly laid out stacks of bills and coins, breaking the hundred up into change that Jim could play with. It included forty one dollar silver and gold coins.

Lawton dealt, five card stud, and Jim won the pot with a pair of sevens and an ace high. On the next game a second man dropped out and left hurriedly.

When he was gone, Jim took his sixgun, spun the cylinder and looked at Lawton.

'Our usual rules?' Jim asked.

Lawton took out his Derringer and laid it on the table near his right hand as Jim put down his .44. 'Yes, Mr. Steel, our usual rules.'

The remaining miner was in his late forties, knew cards and card players and was good. He stared a moment at the two guns, decided it

139

was none of his business and began shuffling the cards.

They played for almost two hours, and when the third man bowed out, Lawton closed the game.

'You have too much good luck tonight, Steel. I'd rather save your heavy money for a time when Lady Luck is favoring me.'

Jim put the money away in his pocket, then changed his mind and sold a hundred dollars' worth back to Lawton for his hundred dollar bill, and slid his .44 into his leather home.

'Always a pleasure to do business with you, Mr. Lawton. We'll have to do this more often.'

On his way back to camp, Jim walked in the shadows and stayed well away from blazing campfires. He figured he had relieved Lawton's purse of just over two hundred dollars. Not a bad night's work.

When Jim slid down beside the glowing embers in the pit fire at his camp, Lucas had company. Chow Ling sat before the fire. He saw Jim, stood quickly and bowed, offered him his seat by the fire and stepped back chattering softly in Mandarin. Lucas held up a hand and the singsong Chinese language stopped.

'Chow Ling is with us, as you can see. He says that you saved his life tonight, and he is grateful. He wishes you could also have saved his wife. However now, according to ancient Chinese law, he belongs to you because you saved him. I have been trying to talk him out of

140

it for two hours. He cooked up some sweet plums for us, and made some biscuits right here over the fire with a little reflector thing he had on the wagon. But he says he's going to stay with you, and live here and work for you.'

'Tell him we'll pay him for everything he lost today,' Jim said. 'Mr. Lawton's gambling losses will cover the bill.'

'Tarnation, Jim, don't you hear too good no more? This here Chink says he belongs to you, as in ownership. He says he's your slave for the rest of his life.'

'Sure, Lucas, right. I'm too tired tonight even to think about that. Tell Chow to stand guard tonight and we'll talk about it tomorrow. Can he use a sixgun?'

'Sure can. They shot one out of his hand, but...'

'No buts, Lucas. I'm beat, finished, done in. That poker playing is harder work than I remembered. That's why I gave up the profession.'

Jim crawled under his blankets, realized it wasn't as cold tonight as it had been last night and then saw Chow Ling leaning against a pine tree with a sixgun in his hand. Then Jim drifted to sleep, a peaceful deep sleep where he dreamed he was $200 richer and a furious H. William Lawton was standing beside a midget who screamed meaningless words at Jim.

## CHAPTER ELEVEN

# THE FIRST TUNNEL

Jim woke to the smell of bacon, eggs, flapjacks, and coffee. He sat up and kicked off his blankets, pulled on his boots and laced them up. By then he got his eyes open enough to see Chow Ling working over the cooking fire.

The small Chinese smiled, bowed, and pointed at a small folding table and two chairs that sat to one side.

'Breakfast plenty ready,' he said and bowed again.

The table was set for two, with china dishes, delicate china cups and silverware. Each plate had a small linen mat, a glass of water, and a cup of steaming coffee. Lucas occupied one chair and shoveled a square of hotcake into his mouth.

'Come and get it before I eat it all,' he said.

Jim washed his face in the stream, then sat down to a stack of four big hotcakes, with three over-easy eggs on top, a cup of hot maple syrup on the side and another cup filled with steaming coffee. Jim sipped the coffee. It was the best he'd had in months. The flapjacks tasted like they had been made with milk. Just then a raucous, bawling moo sounded behind him and Jim turned to find a brown-eyed

Jersey cow staring at him.

'A cow?' Jim yelped.

'True,' Lucas said. 'Chow Ling led her up here tied to the back of his wagon. He didn't think there would be one here. He's as sharp as a new-honed razor.'

Jim settled down to his breakfast. He held up his cup for more coffee and Chow Ling ran with it, the coffee came from a blue enameled coffee pot without a single chip on it. Jim took the coffee then held up a finger.

'Chow Ling, we've got to talk. I'll pay you ten dollars a week to be our cook. Is that enough?'

'No pay. Belong Jim Steel.'

Jim ignored it. 'And besides the ten dollars a week, I owe you for all the food and equipment you brought in. You and Lucas figure out a fair price for it and I'll pay for it. We'll put it in the log cabin Lucas is putting up. Until then you be guard.'

'No buy. Chow Ling give Jim Steel. Now, much busy.' The small Chinaman with the long black pigtail down his back returned to his fire. Jim saw that he was baking something. He had produced a reflector oven and a large iron cooking pot. The pot went in the reflector area opposite the heat and the loaf of bread went in the pot. Jim saw another reflector directly on the other side of the fire. All Jim could do was shake his head and sip at the coffee. He'd work out some kind of arrangement with the man.

143

He must have had his entire life's savings invested in the wagon, the horses, the cow, and the merchandise.

Lucas hired two more men that morning, put one in charge of building the log cabin, and then supervised. They had two rows of logs laid down now, notched and in place. Lucas had left a three foot wide door in the center, facing the stream, and space for one window on the short end. On the other end one of the men was ready to start a stone fireplace, but there was no mortar or cement. Lucas thought he'd seen some adobe clay downstream when he was fishing one day. He took his horse and rode down to find the spot.

That morning Jim found Johnny Johnson before he got in the cold water.

'How's the leg coming along?'

Johnson grinned. 'Didn't think you was ever gonna ask me. I don't swing a pick none too good no more, but there's other things I can do.'

'Good. I found out Ted McIntosh did have a wife. So that thousand dollars you found belongs to her. She's a partner in the mine.'

'Good, now when do I go to work?'

'Right now. Just as soon as you can get your gear moved up to the claim. Put your stuff near the wagon with the rest of us, and tell Lucas you're eating with us from now on. Chow Ling won't mind another mouth to feed.'

Back at the claim, Jim asked Chow Ling if he

144

had a pick and shovel. The small man beamed.

'Six.' He trotted to the wagon and brought back two of each type.

Jim thanked him and took the tools up to the face of his claim. He swung the pick at the wall and was surprised to find the point sink four inches into the cliff. It wasn't nearly as hard as he thought it might be. Lots of loose quartz and some harder rock.

With the pick he outlined the size of the tunnel around the exposed vein. The niche in the wall provided him with a dozen feet of flat area before he came to the stream. There would be some space here to store a little ore he dug before he got the bridge in and the rail cars all ready. They might be able to use a wagon before then to ford the stream.

Jim paused and stared at the gold ore. Was it worth the trouble? He had come up here to find a killer, not to strike a bonanza. But now he was making an investment for Ted's widow, which was almost as important. Yes, it was worth finding out just how good the ore was. He stepped up and started swinging the pick again.

Before noon, Jim had made a good start on the tunnel. It was seven feet high and eight feet wide at the front. He had shoveled the worthless rock and gravel to one side, but carefully piled the ore-bearing quartz to the other side where he could load it later. He sat on the mound and looked at the quartz. It didn't look like gold, not yet. It didn't even sparkle. The refining process took care of that. Jim stared at a fist full of the ore. Was it going to produce $20 or $200 a ton? Jim grinned. That was part of the big gamble, the ever-present bonanza they all looked for, even he. He knew the ore was rich, it would be worth mining.

Would the Utes give them any trouble when they saw the miners were digging into the middle of the rock they claimed as a sacred burial ground? Probably.

Just after lunch, Jim took two of Lucas's men and the cross-cut saw and built a temporary bridge. They felled four two-foot thick trees, trimmed them and with a horse dragged twenty-foot lengths of the pine logs to the creek, then laid them across from bank to bank. They were straight enough that they lay securely side by side, made a serviceable bridge. They would put rocks in the cracks and then fill it over with dirt to make a smooth surface. Later they would put planks over it.

Jim had the men sink the trimmed tops of the trees in the downstream bank as pillings, digging the holes deep, then planting the foot-thick poles in the holes and filling around them with rocks and rammed earth. With posts on all four corners of the bridge and eventually the posts cabled together, Jim hoped the spring floods would not wash it away.

He sent the saw back to the log cabin
146

workers, and then discovered that Chow Ling had brought two saws in his wagon. Jim used one to start cutting timbers to be used for a square-set bracing for the mine tunnels. He wanted the mine to be the safest one ever dug. The quartz ore was not as hard here as in some places, and since they had hit no hard rock, he was a little worried about cave-ins. Around the face of the tunnel he put up a foot thick log frame. The tunnel was still only a dent in the face of the cliff so far, barely a foot deep. Jim had left the floor of the tunnel a foot above the river bank. He hoped that the slope of the tunnel would be a slight incline going in, so the loaded ore cars would be rolled down the slope coming out.

They were lucky that afternoon. One of the men sawing down a tree for square sets on the slope above the mine tunnel saw the Indians coming. He had been resting when they slipped along the slope below him well inside the heavy timber. He saw them first, which had probably saved his life. His name was Judson Bailey and he got off six shots at the closest brave, missed with all six, and then ran like a rabid rabbit toward the mine.

As soon as the men in camp heard the shots they dove for cover and for their weapons, splashed out of the stream and levered rifle rounds into place and full-cocked sixguns.

The Indians were at a disadvantage from the start. Jim wiped sweat from his hat as he looked around a log waiting to be cut into lengths for square sets and braces. He saw a brave slide behind a tree in the woods above and sighted in on the far side of the tree. When the savage's head eased out for a look around the pine, Jim fired. The round hit the tree and the head vanished.

When the first attack came, Jim had three men at the tunnel, and four working on the cabin. The men panning gold were spread along the creek. There was no concentration of men for a hail of arrows this time, but bowstrings twanged and the two miners were hit by arrows early in the fracas.

Three Indians rushed the men at the log cabin site. One Ute took a .45 slug through the chest, a second caught a bullet in the shoulder. The three managed to set off half a dozen arrows as they ran and the only miner wounded was Lucas, whose arm an arrow had grazed. It was his greatest war wound and he would tout it forever. Now he grumbled at the lucky shot, broke the arrow in half, and threw it at the Indian.

Jim had taken his rifle to the tunnel with him this time, and now he began working his way downstream so he could see the main party of miners. He had been around the small bend in the creek which cut off his view. He gained a log near the bend and glanced over it.

The Indians had chosen to come through the woods in back of the miners' camps this time, evidently hoping for a surprise attack. The lumberjack had disrupted their plans. Jim leveled the Ballard .56 caliber over the log and watched the brush. He was far out of effective arrow range. But his big Ballard was still on short target distance. He saw a movement well above the camp. He watched it again, then in the shadows made out an arm. Jim sighted in to the left of the arm where he guessed the body would be. He aimed again and fired. When the puff of smoke from the end of his rifle blew away, Jim saw the brush clearly again. An Indian screamed, raised halfway on his knees, then fell to the ground.

The sound of the heavy rifle brought another spate of firing into the timber by the miners. Jim felt sure most of them didn't have targets, but it was a highly effective method to discourage the attackers. The shooting tapered off and the wood fell quiet.

'They vamoosed?' someone asked.

'Don't see nary a one,' another voice came.

'Just hold on a little, and be sure,' Lucas yelled. 'We ain't got nowhere to go no way.'

The woods settled down again. A blue jay scolded off to the right. A bobcat yowled somewhere across the stream. Jim scanned the woods as he did on a military patrol, seeing nothing, watching everything, noticing the faintest movement. He saw one form fade toward a tree, pause, then move to another pine—a moment later the Indian was lost in thick foliage. The last of the braves had pulled out.

'All clear,' Jim called five minutes later. 'I think we beat them back. Anybody hurt?'

Nobody would admit it if he was, so any wounds must be miner, Jim decided. The men slowly went back to work, and this time each carried a sixgun and many had loaded rifles close to hand.

Four men didn't start panning again. They packed their gear and got ready to leave. One big Swede shook his head. 'Hell, I pan out an ounce of gold in two days, it's more than I'd make in two weeks working the mine. But the yellow is gone here. So I got to move on to a new spot where the yellow is fresh. I'm not a hard-rock man. I don't like tunnels and holes. Besides, it's getting too cold up here and the Utes are getting too bold. Always wanted to try my luck in them warm Arizona mountains. Why does gold only come in cold places?'

Jim watched the man go, then walked back to the tunnel. He had to do something about the Indians. He didn't know what. Bailey who saw them first said there were eight of them, all braves but some seemed young.

That's when Jim remembered his army days in the big war. The three men working at the face of the tunnel were all back by the time he got there.

'Any of you men ever serve in the army?' he asked. 'Either side?'

150

A man of about thirty raised his hand. 'I did, Captain. What you got in mind?'

His name was Andrews and he had claimed hard-rock experience. Andrews was a little taller than most of the men.

'How would you like to pull guard duty for a week or so? Take a rifle and two sixguns and post yourself where you can watch for the Indians. They might not come back, but we should have out some security.'

'Hell yes, Captain. Beats using a shovel.'

'You'll be on your own. You go to sleep or get careless, and you're liable to lose your scalp.'

'Know that, Captain. Where do you want me?'

'Where do you think you should be?'

Andrews looked around. 'They came down the river first time, from the other side. Then they attacked through the woods behind. If they do it again, I'd guess it'd be from across the river. Better cover there, easier to get away.'

'Sounds good, Andrews. You have a rifle?'

Andrews nodded.

'They won't be back today, so you get a good night's sleep. I want you in your position at dawn. Take some food with you and come back at four in the afternoon.'

'Same pay?' Andrews asked.

'No hazard pay. Twelve dollars a week, Andrews.'

'Good.'

That night around the campfire, Jim noticed changes. Chow had built a better fire ring, utilized his own reflectors to make the cooking fire more efficient, and proudly served them homemade bread. It was a little heavy, but still delicious. The small folding table had been expanded and now could seat three. Chow had jerry-rigged some wooden boxes and made a chair from a two-foot high round of a foot-thick log.

The supply wagon had been pulled closer to the fire and a tarp extended over the wagon and serving table. It would keep the sun off them and some of the rain.

After a meal of mashed potatoes, beef steak, brown gravy made with milk, real butter and homemade bread, Jim leaned back in comfort before the fire.

'I'm not even going to ask where the steak came from,' Jim said.

Lucas grinned. 'He brought it from Durango, froze it before he left and kept it in some ice during the day. Don't ask me where he found that much ice.'

Jim motioned Chow Ling over. He came quickly.

'Chow Ling, where did you learn to cook so well?'

'Ah. San Francisco. Big house. Rich man. Very bad man who own Chow Ling before.'

'Owned you?'

152

'Yes, Chow Ling and wife.'

'Then how did you get here?'

Chow Ling smiled, looked at his fire, and his small kitchen that had sprouted under the tarp. 'Long story. Must go now.' He took the plates from the table and ran back to his kitchen.

That night Jim waited until the talk around the fire died down, then he looked up at Johnny Johnson and Lucas. 'How would you two gentlemen like to file claims on a potential hard-rock mine?'

Lucas looked up. 'You're saying you're not sure where the vein might wander?'

'Exactly. It's got a fifty-fifty chance of meandering either way and off my six-hundred foot frontage.'

Johnny burped and then took another drink of coffee. 'Seems reasonable. What if the vein turns my way?'

'Then we'd have to dicker some,' Jim said. 'Or you could file on it, then sell your claim rights to me for a dollar.'

'If I was stupid I could. Let's say if it does come on my claim, I get ten percent of the net return from my ore.'

Jim nodded. 'Thought I picked the right man. I understand you also know how to set up books and make them work. You draw up the agreements, same for you and Lucas, and tomorrow we'll go out and stake your claims. One on the lower side will be along the far side of the river in back of the panning claims. But that should still keep us covered. No problem with the upriver side.'

They all shook hands.

'We should have a drink to celebrate,' Johnny said.

Lucas sent a warning glance at Jim.

'Right, Johnny, a drink, but just one because we've got a lot of important work to do tomorrow.'

Sure enough, Chow Ling found a pint of whiskey in his wagon, and poured an inch of straight booze into each cup. The men toasted the new mine, the Devil's Gulch Bonanza.

Jim lay on his blankets a half hour later. Something was bothering him and he couldn't shake it. The sullen, worrisome feeling down deep that he wasn't working hard enough to find Ted McIntosh's killers. He argued that he had to get the mine going first, and he knew that such an excuse could be used for at least a year. He had to do something now, first thing tomorrow. He had to track down the only two leads he had, or that he thought he had.

One was the storekeeper. How did Lindstrom get his money to put up a cabin and open a store? The other lead was the gambler. Lawton seemed such an obvious villain Jim tended to overlook him. No gambler was going to kill somebody just to get back some losses. And surely not if he would need help to do the deed.

Jim thought about that. He decided good

help for a murder might not be too hard to find in Devil's Gulch.

Jim worried about it for half an hour. Then he made up his mind what he would do, turned over, and went to sleep at once.

## CHAPTER TWELVE

## BRAND NEW GIRL IN TOWN

Jim woke the next morning as eager to get going as he could remember. A brand new venture! A new mine to test, to develop, to work! And a new approach to his search for Ted's killer.

Breakfast was biscuits and gravy, and large bowls of cooked oatmeal with sugar and milk. The three men showed their appreciation by eating every last scrap of food, and then each bowed formally to the little Chinese before going to work.

Jim headed for the general store, took back the cross cut he had borrowed and, when the customer in the store left, went up to Abe Lindstrom.

'Abe, I need your help.'

The store manager looked sideways at Jim, then scowled. 'Lots of folks up here need my help. I might be able to oblige, just so it don't cost me no money and no time.'

'Shouldn't. You remember a guy by the name of Ted McIntosh? He's about my age, big man, quiet, had a blazing bush of red hair.'

'Oh, him. Yeah, I remember him. He ain't been around for a while. Gone I guess.'

'Right, gone. He's dead. Murdered right here in Devil's Gulch.' Jim watched Lindstrom. He was either very good at lying or knew nothing about the killing.

'Murdered? Now that's a dangerous word to use in a mining camp. But, you being on the Miner's Committee and being our lawman, guess you can say it.' Abe took out a plug of tobacco, chawed off a piece and mixed it up some before he pushed it into the wad already in his right cheek. 'Yeah, I heard something about it being strange that a big man like him would get knocked out and drown under his own little sluice. But nobody brought no charges. You know we got to have charges.'

Jim stared at Lindstrom, trying to make up his mind how hard he should play his hand. 'Abe, that man was one of my best friends. I came up here for one reason, to find the killer and gut-shoot him, or maybe put one round into each of his knees first, so the killer will understand what pain is all about before he dies. I don't give a damn who it is, Abe. You or old Lucas, that preacher Committee chairman, or even the gambler. I'm here to get him and if he's smart he'll either get out of camp, or make a play for me. Either way is fine with me. I thought you might want to pass the word. Law and order have come to Devil's Gulch, and come to stay!'

Abe looked him in the eye. 'That's a mighty hard line you're taking, Steel. McIntosh is dead and gone, you had nothing to do with it. Let it lay. That mine you got up there now, that's another matter. It could be a good one. I seen the ore. Why put everything on the line for one shot of vengeance? You're a smart man, Steel. You know what that mother lode could be worth. Gunning down somebody won't bring McIntosh back, and it could be the end of you.'

'I pay my debts, Abe. Ted would have done this for me. Besides, he's got a widow. She'll want to know what happened, and what I did about it.'

Abe's face mellowed just a little. 'Steel, the man you want might be long gone from here. More'n three dozen men have been in and out of camp since McIntosh died. How you know he's even here now? Ease off, work your mine, make a fortune, and let's have a thriving community here. Then I'll make some money too.'

'Thanks for the advice, still you pass the word. Him against me, anytime.'

Jim turned and left the store. He jogged up the hill to the mine, eager now to get to work. He knew he had touched a nerve somewhere with Abe Lindstrom. He wasn't sure why, but

157

there had been a nervous flutter of one eye, a small muscle tightening, just enough. Lindstrom might not even notice he reacted, but he did. He knew something that he wasn't talking about. Jim also figured this was the last time he showed his back to any man in camp. He'd keep away from the fire at night, sleep in the brush, he wouldn't make it easy for a killer to bushwhack him. He wasn't afraid of a fair fight, even a walk-down.

The new mine tunnel looked about the same. Two men worked at the task of removing the worthless rock at the bottom of the new hole. When he got there they let Jim use the pick to break down the gold ore, then they shoveled it to one side.

'What's the bet?' Jim asked. 'Is it going to be ten dollars a ton and not worth taking out, or will it be a bonanza at two-hundred a ton?'

That started them talking as they worked for the rest of the morning. In the end they decided to start a pool. Each man would bet $20 worth of gold dust or a double-eagle, and put in his guess how much a ton the ore would assay out. The one guessing the closest got the pot.

'And we have Lucas hold our money and write down the guess,' one of the workers said.

'Let's let it go to the closest fifty cents, like $145.50 per ton.'

Jim let them talk it out. They worked hard, shoveling away the dregs on one side, keeping the gold-bearing ore to the other. Soon it was evident that the vein was turning slightly to the right. They had the tunnel three feet into the hillside now, and a big pile of worthless rock and dirt on one side that almost filled the small ledge. It was about as much as they could dig until they figured out a way to move the useless sand and rock.

'What about Lucas's old wagon and that donkey of his?' one the the men asked. 'We could back the wagon up there on the bridge, carry out the dirt and dump it in, then haul it away, maybe up on the shelf.'

Jim decided to use the first loads of dirt to build up a solid roadway along the timber edge of the ravine, one that he hoped wouldn't wash out in the spring runoff.

Then it was noon and he had just started to talk to Lucas about it when a whoop and a yell went up as another load of supplies came in from Durango. A dozen pistols let loose and everyone ran for the general store.

Jim went with the others and stopped short when he saw the small scene at the store. Two shotgun guards stood beside a woman who sat on the wagon seat. He moved closer and saw that she was young and pretty with shoulder-length blond hair. One of the guards fired his shotgun into the air and yelled at the men to quiet down.

'Any of you gents here know one Jim Steel? This young lady has come ahunting him and if one hair on her head gets harmed, you'll be answering to my shotgun. You got a Jim Steel here?'

The men nodded and Jim walked slowly toward the wagon. He had no idea what this was about. He was sure that he had never seen the girl before in his life. Then he smiled and ran forward. He knew who she must be.

'Mrs. McIntosh, what in the world are you doing way out here?'

She glanced at him in surprise. 'Jim? Jim Steel?' she asked. She rose and then sat down quickly, blinking back tears. 'They said you'd come here. I tried to find you in Denver, but you had left there. Your banker told me you went to Durango, and there they said you had come up here. I've very glad to find you.'

Jim turned to the men who had quieted and stood staring at the prettiest woman they had seen in months. Some of them hadn't seen a female in a year.

'Gentlemen, may I present Mrs. Naomi McIntosh the widow of the late Ted McIntosh who lies buried over on the hill.'

There was a buzzing in the crowd, then Jim helped Naomi down and led her toward the store.

Abe motioned them inside. He was busy inspecting his goods. The clerk smiled and bowed and said they could talk privately in the store. He went to the porch.

Naomi McIntosh hadn't said a word more until they were through the door. Jim leaned

160

against the counter and watched her. She was beautiful, with soft clear skin, darting blue eyes, the long blond hair framing an oval face with slightly pouting lips. She wore a heavy coat but he could tell by the way she walked that she was trim and slender. She noticed his evaluation and lifted her brows.

'Sorry if I was staring, but beautiful women are a rare commodity up here. You're only the second woman ever in Devil's Gulch.' He smiled. 'Yes, you're the kind of girl Ted would marry, I can see that. A real beauty, with all the good looks in the world, and a heap of brains and enough spunk to outclaw a wildcat and eat him for breakfast.'

She smiled and looked down. A blush showed at her cheeks, and when she glanced back at him there was another redness, but now it was in her eyes as quick tears flowed.

'Somebody killed Ted, didn't they? Isn't that why you came up here, to find out who it was?'

Jim folded his arms. 'Yes, Naomi, I'm positive that somebody murdered Ted, but so far I haven't been able to find out who or why, but I have some leads. Right now that can wait. You're more important now. You did a very brave, dangerous and foolish thing coming up here. It's a two day drive in a wagon...'

She waved it away with a hand with long delicate fingers. 'Don't worry about that, I was as safe as a church. One of the shotgun guards is the Baptist preacher from Durango. He'd

161

have skinned alive either of the men if they'd tried to touch me.'

'But here it's even more dangerous. A Chinese woman was raped and killed up here only a few days ago. She came in unannounced with her husband and before some of us could get down here...'

'But I've found you, Jim. You can protect me. Ted told me so much about you, the places you'd been, the scrapes, the good times. Sometimes I thought you were right there living with us. But soon I realized that it was a long friendship built and tested through danger and action and mutual trust. That's why I knew that you would do something about that news item I put in the Denver paper. But by the time I got to Denver I was too late, you'd left.'

'Naomi, you can't stay here. You must know that, it's too primitive, too hard, and winter's coming.'

'That's what Mr. Borcherding told me. He's the preacher with the shotgun. But I told him I had to see you, to talk to you. I had to know for sure what happened to Ted.'

'You'll stay here tonight, then we'll ride out first thing in the morning. One long day's ride and we can get the forty miles to Durango.'

'Forty miles, on a horse, in one day?'

'Can you ride?'

'I've been riding since I was ten.'

'Good, you can do it. First let me bring you

up to date. I'm not sure exactly what happened to Ted. But I do know that while he was here he discovered a gold mine upstream, and I think it's the mother lode for this placer mining. That means there's a gold mine upstream that I've got staked. But since Ted found it first, it's his mine too. That makes it your mine and since I had to find it again, it's part mine too. You have fifty percent of the Devil's Gulch Bonanza, whether it peters out in ten feet or whether it's a million dollar a year producer. Later I'll take you up to look at your mine.'

She took off the little hat that had been restricting the blond hair and shook her head to fluff up her hair. It was a natural move, so feminine that Jim stared openly. He hadn't seen anything that interesting in months. He smiled now as he watched her, impressed again that she was such a pretty girl.

'Jim, slow down just a little. You have a real hard-rock mine up here?'

'Yes, and you own half. We'll go up and look it over soon. There also are Indians around here, and we've been attacked twice, but I don't think they'll be back.' He paused and watched her. 'Naomi, you understand that you can't stay here, don't you?'

'Yes, I can see that ... now. It isn't much of a town is it? One log cabin and twenty tents.'

'You're right, Naomi. It isn't much of a town ... yet. But it could be. The gold panning is about finished here, and we're just starting to open the mine. I've got six or seven men working now. Ted left a thousand dollars in paper money that his killers overlooked, and we're using some of that for payroll along with the gold dust we've panned.'

She was ahead of him. 'But you'll need machinery, equipment, heavy things, and rails, ore cars. I'm a mining engineer's daughter, I've lived around mines half of my life in one state or another.'

'Good. Then you really understand how wild a camp is at this time. We have to get you back to Durango tomorrow.'

'I guess so. But I'd love to be in on the opening of the new mine, especially one that Ted found.'

'You will be, on most of it. Let's find Borcherding and I'll take you on the grand tour before it gets dark. With Borcherding and my sixgun we shouldn't have any trouble. Then I'm hoping that Abe Lindstrom will let us use his room here in back tonight.'

Outside the store the men had melted away, but they stopped working and watched when Jim and Mrs. McIntosh walked by. Jim talked to Abe briefly. He nodded and then Jim went back to Naomi as Borcherding watched and they moved up the stream bank.

They walked quickly along the creek, passing several campfires and small tents as they went to Jim's camp. He introduced Naomi to Lucas and Johnson who were waiting. They gave her a cup of coffee and she said she was surprised how good it was. Chow Ling bowed to her and promised her a special treat for lunch. Then the three of them went up to the mine entrance.

'There's not much to see yet,' Jim said. 'But right up here I found rock hammer marks that no one but Ted could have made.' They walked across the bridge. 'There it is, the first tunnel in the fantastic Devil's Gulch Bonanza Gold Mine.'

She stopped and stared at it. 'Somehow I have the feeling that Ted approves, that he knows you found his mine and he wants you—us—to make a success of it. I can't say why I feel that way.' She caught his arm and held it tightly. 'Let's—go over and sample that pile of gold ore.'

A few moments later she reached down and took a handful of the quartz ore and studied it. She ground it through her fingers and smiled, even as a tear worked its way down her pale white cheek.

'Yes, Mr. Steel. I think your friend Mr. McIntosh is happy at this moment, and I'm sure he's going to help us in every way that he can.' She let go of his arm then and stepped into the small tunnel and tried to smile.

'What's your guess on the assay report,' she said.

'Want in our pool? For twenty dollars you can take a guess.'

'What was your guess, Jim?'

'A hundred and ninety dollars a ton.'

'That's high. The vein is turning, you know.'

'Yes.'

'How much frontage did you say, six hundred feet?'

'Yes ... federal mining laws. How did you know that?'

'I told you I'm a mining engineer's daughter. You're bound to pick up something about the business after so many years.' She stopped and looked at him closely with her clear blue eyes. 'How did you know my name back at the wagon? I never told anyone I was coming. Ted never wrote to you that he had married. How did you know?'

'I figured anyone crazy enough to marry Ted McIntosh would also be crazy enough to risk her life and limb coming up to where her husband was last seen alive.'

'Honestly? You thought that?'

'Partly. And then I read your name in Ted's family Bible. We found it with his things. I've got it for you.'

'Thank you, Jim, you're a good and true friend. Ted was right about you.'

'The Irish always exaggerate.'

Her eyes smiled at him, then she sobered. 'Then you know when we married ... such a short time.' She shivered and looked away from the mine, then stepped out of the tunnel. 'Where are your boundaries, *our* boundaries?

166

Do you have any back up claims alongside?'

Jim chuckled at her understanding of the business, and pointed out the frontage stakes and the eleven hundred feet running well up into the mountain behind them.

'So altogether we have eighteen hundred feet by eleven hundred feet. That's about a third of a mile one way, and a fifth of a mile the other. It should do unless you have found one of a whole group of veins.'

She looked across the river into the woods and where the log cabin was having its fourth row of logs put on. 'We haven't much room for buildings and equipment and the stamping mill, do we. Where will the stamper go?'

Jim pointed out the spot and she nodded. 'Yes, as close as practical to the mine entrance. Rail cars of course, hand pushed or with donkeys?'

'Hand pushed if the vein cooperates. We're hoping it will go slightly uphill from the entrance.'

'Veins often have a way of failing to cooperate, though, don't they?' She paused and looked around. 'It was terribly cold last night. How far away are we from the first snowfall?'

'I'd guess two months, unless we have an early winter.'

'Any housing for the men?'

Jim showed her where he wanted the barracks type building for the men. It would be logs too, forty feet by twenty feet, divided into two big rooms with logs in the middle. He turned her back toward the camp. 'I didn't know I was getting such an expert in mining when I wrote you in as a partner. You're going to be a big help.'

'Then I can stay?'

He shook his head. 'In the spring when things are a little more settled down, and we have a stable crew and some law and order. Maybe then.'

'I won't accept fifty percent. That's far too much. I might go along with twenty percent, if you convince me, and especially if I can help in the work. You actually have no proof that Ted found this spot. He probably did. He told me he was coming up here to try to find the mother lode. If he did he'd try to raise enough money to put it into production. Is there a gambler in camp?'

Jim smiled. 'You knew your man pretty well, didn't you? Yes there is a gambler, and he could be the killer, I don't know yet. It's my guess Ted found the vein, then began gambling with Lawton to try to double his bankroll so he could hire some good men. Then he'd stake out his hard rock claim, start to work it and leave it in the hands of someone he trusted while he rode out to find enough money to get the mine underway in force. Somebody stopped him before he got that far.'

'Jim, don't talk about that part.'

168

He watched the instant tears in her eyes. She sniffled and wiped them.

'You said ... you said there was a grave?'

'I asked. They didn't mark it. No way to make a marker that would last very long up here. I'm sorry.'

Tears now flooded down her cheeks. She reached out and held his arm again, tightly, pressing against him for support and courage. 'Let's get back to your camp.'

They walked slowly, Borcherding in back, watching, the shotgun at the ready at all times. In Jim's camp, Chow Ling had set the little table for two.

'Both hungry, eat,' he said. Jim was never sure where the Chinaman got the food, but he put Borcherding and Naomi at the table fixed with the faint blue china and brought out a beef stew, fresh bread and butter and glasses of milk. For dessert there were small cakes and sliced canned peaches.

Borcherding ate quickly, then stood in his guard pose while Naomi finished her lunch. When she was through she shook Chow Ling's hand.

'That was the best lunch I've had in weeks,' she said. 'And out here in the wilderness with no equipment ... It's a miracle.'

Jim led the way back to the store, and saw that Abe Lindstrom had moved most of his personal things out of the living quarters in the far end of the store.

He had even made up the bed with sheets. It was the only bed in all of Devil's Gulch and had a real straw mattress.

Borcherding looked over the area, saw that the only door was in the front, and nodded, sitting down next to it, his shotgun in his arm.

'Mrs. McIntosh must stay inside the store as soon as it gets dark,' Borcherding said. 'I promised to take care of her, so she must stay inside.'

Jim agreed. 'After dark, I'll have Chow Ling bring over some supper for both of you,' Jim said. 'Then I have to talk again to Mrs. McIntosh. Will you be riding back with us tomorrow?'

Borcherding shook his head. 'Nope. Resting up a day here, then driving the wagon back. Probably take us three days since we won't be rushing.'

Jim thanked him and left, going back to the mine and helping the men push the empty eight-foot wagon with eighteen-inch sideboards on the bridge. The rocks and dirt in the crevices between the logs held and the wagon sat there empty and ready.

As they started to move the dirt by hand, Jim realized the masses of equipment he needed, and that he would even have to buy freight wagons to haul it in from Durango, and probably some of it from Denver. Tons and tons of equipment.

For a moment it overwhelmed him. He

watched the men carrying the dirt and rock by the shovel full. It would take a year that way. He ran back to his camp and brought up two canvases he used for ground cloths.

Jim put one canvas on the ground and shoveled it full of dirt and rocks, then with the other men picked it up by the corners and the canvas and carried it to the wagon, boosting it over the side and emptied it. They could move the dirt and rocks ten times as fast that way.

The men worked until dark, then they went to camp. Jim's dinner was waiting. He was so tired he hardly knew what he ate.

'Chow Ling took a mess of food down to Mrs. McIntosh,' Lucas said. 'She said she wants to talk to you as soon as you're through working.'

''Pears as though I'm never going to be done working here.'

'True, young man, true. We put another row of logs up on the cabin, all notched in and solid. Even found some red clay that will fire well so we can use it for mortar in the fireplace to hold the rocks together. Once we get that clay fired hot it'll set up like cement.'

Jim frowned.

'Don't fret about it, Jim. It's going to work. I've done it before. We'll just build a fire in the firebox as we're putting the thing up. First the firebox of red bricks we'll fire. Then we do a layer of rocks and fire it for half a day. Do another layer and fire her again. It works. Not as good as a cement or mortar job, but it should last for twenty years.'

Jim was so tired he couldn't see straight. He walked down the trail, trying to be careful. He hoped the pretty Mrs. McIntosh didn't give him any trouble. She could if she tried. Jim hoped that she didn't. He had all the trouble for one day he could handle.

## CHAPTER THIRTEEN

## WIDOW NAOMI McINTOSH

By the time Jim got to the general store he felt a little better. Just the idea of talking with a pretty girl perked him up and he found Borcherding and his shotgun sitting guard on the front step.

Jim paused and nodded at the Baptist preacher.

'You really interested in protecting that lady?' Jim asked.

'Yeah, of course,' Borcherding said.

'You're a dead goose sitting out here. One shot from the brush and you're dead and the door is left unguarded. Why not go inside the store and lock the door. Then she's got protection and so have you.'

'Wouldn't be proper.'

'There's probably a lock on the living

quarters door.'

'Oh, well, then ... yeah, that would be all right.'

Naomi peeked out.

'Jim?'

'Yes.'

She opened the door and he stepped inside. The store was closed and dark except for one kerosene lamp. She led the way through the goods and tables to the counter, around it and into a room at the back lighted by two coal oil lamps. The room was eight feet wide and the width of the store, about twelve feet. A bed in the far end was made up with a hand quilted comforter. A rocking chair and table and a few wall shelves completed the sparse furnishings. A round potbellied cast iron stove huddled against the wall and glowed hotly with a wood fire.

She waved her hand at the room. 'It's cozy, and so much better than sleeping on that old wagon.'

He stared at her. Jim had not seen her with her bulky coat off. She wore a long sleeved print dress with a collar high around her neck, and the skirt just cleared the floor. But it couldn't camouflage the swell of her breasts and her pinched in waist.

She noticed him staring and smiled. 'Now, Jim. I know it hasn't been a year since you've seen a woman. Admit it.'

Jim grinned embarrassment. 'Yes, I've seen

173

girls since then, but none as beautiful as you are, Mrs. McIntosh.'

She smiled, seemed to fight down the beginning of a blush, and sat on the bed. 'Jim, I want to be honest with you. I like you and I guess I was fishing a little for a compliment. But it's been a long time since a man has said nice things to me.' She took a big breath. 'Now that I've made my small confession, I want to try to convince you that I can stay here. Jim, I can shoot a sixgun, my father taught me. I can help get the mine going in lots of ways...' She stopped when she saw his frown.

Jim spoke softly but with an intensity that she felt deeply.

'Naomi. You lost your husband up here, and Ted could take care of himself as well as any man I know. I saw the brutality of this camp just last week when that Chinese woman was attacked, gang-raped, and strangled. I never want to see a woman go through anything like that again. I'm sorry, Naomi, this is one point I won't argue about. I won't even talk about it again. There is absolutely no way I'll allow you to stay here until we get some buildings up, establish some stability of the people here, and get an orderly society built.'

'Yes, Jim. All right, I understand. I had to ask once more. Now sit down in the rocking chair, we've got a lot of things to talk about.' She sat on the edge of the bed.

Jim dropped into the chair, and wiped his
174

hand across his face. 'Naomi, I didn't mean to be unkind, but I know what mining camps can be like in the first days. I just couldn't live with myself if anything happened to you up here.'

'Yes, Jim, I understand. Now, what about your financing? How much is it going to take to get this project into production? Will twenty-five thousand dollars do it?'

Jim leaned back and relaxed. He hadn't met many women who knew anything about business matters or really cared. Quickly he found himself detailing his plans for the mine, where he would raise the financing, his trip to Denver, his banker, how he thought he could get a stamping mill brought in at a good price. Before he realized it the time had gotten away.

'Jim, if we're getting an early start, we should get some rest.'

He stood. 'I did get a little wound up, didn't I? This is a project that I want to see go right.'

'I understand.'

'Did you bring a valise, any baggage?' he asked.

'Just what I put in my pockets.'

'Good, traveling light, I like that. I'll come by for you about a half hour after daylight. I want to load both my saddle bags with gold ore, plenty for a realistic assay.' He smiled down at her and took her hand. Suddenly he wanted to kiss her fingers but he knew he shouldn't. 'I'll see you in the morning. Oh, I suggested to Borcherding that he be on guard inside the store, not out on the step. Is that all right with you?'

'Yes, perfectly fine.'

He nodded once more, realized again what a beautiful woman she was and went out the door.

*　　*　　*

Dawn came crisp and early. Jim had the saddlebags packed before the first sprinkles of light. Chow Ling had fixed breakfast fast and taken it down to Mrs. McIntosh. Jim ate potatoes and onion, bacon and flapjacks, then had a glass of milk and biscuits and real butter. As he swung up on his long time mount, Hamlet, Jim saw Chow Ling come out with a flour sack wrapped and bound carefully. He showed it to Jim, then tied it on the saddle in back of the blanket roll.

'Dinner, dinner,' Chow Ling said and stepped back smiling.

'Thanks, Chow Ling, that's thoughtful of you. Take care of everyone until I get back.'

Chow Ling bowed and Jim rode down through the sleeping camps to the general store.

Naomi McIntosh waited for him, pacing back and forth in front of the store. When she saw him, she mounted the horse Jim had made ready for her the night before, swung into the saddle astride, and arranged her skirts neatly.

176

'I'm ready whenever you are, Mr. Steel.'

'Then, Mrs. McIntosh, let's ride.'

She grinned, jumped her brown into a canter and moved out into the breaking dawn down the trail along the Los Pinos river.

They rode steadily, following the scratch through the wilderness, marked only by a wagon wheel rut here and there, a bent over young conifer tree and a few hoof prints cutting into the sod.

'It's a wonderful morning to be out riding,' Naomi said, looking at him from under the brim of the mannish hat that completely hid her pale blond hair.

'You sound like a traveling person, Mrs. McIntosh. I'd guess after we've sat a saddle for ten hours, both of us will be a little less enthusiastic about riding.'

She smiled and they let the horses walk into the creek, pause and have a drink, then move on across into a stand of pine and some willow. The wagon had mashed down a semblance of a trail here, and they rode for a mile without saying a word. Then she started talking as if she needed to.

'Jim, I only knew Ted for three months before I married him. He warned me that it wouldn't be easy and that I'd be left alone sometimes. But he was such a good man, such a friend, that I knew from the first that I'd marry him if he asked me. We were the best friends, Jim, besides being married. That isn't always the case. My mother never really liked my father. She died a few years ago. Oh, there's one thing you should know about me, Jim. I do tend to chatter away sometimes. If it gets on your nerves, just tell me to be quiet.'

She glanced at him with her soft blue eyes and he laughed.

'Naomi, it's been so long since I've heard the sound of a woman's voice that you'll be hoarse before I tell you to stop.'

They rounded a sharp bend in the Los Pinos, forded it again where it merged with a feeder stream and then the trail dropped steeply for a hundred yards and the horses stepped warily down the slope.

Jim watched her as she rode, wondering if she would be a problem. She said she could ride, and she could, seeming perfectly at home in a saddle. But a woman in a mining camp was always a worry, especially the first few months, and if she were the only woman there. And Naomi was the kind who would want to be there, who would insist on taking part in the development of the mine as soon as she could. Jim would worry about that later.

She had worn the heavy, warm coat that she came up in, and it totally hid the provocative figure, but Jim remembered it well enough from their talk in the store last night. He saw how Ted had been attracted to her. For a moment he wondered what it would be like to kiss her soft lips, to hold her tightly. Then he purged the idea. She was Ted's wife and in mourning, also a business partner; he wasn't going to get into any entanglements like that. Besides she was a lady, not a saloon cutie.

They rode steadily and he never heard a word of complaint or pain from Naomi. She watched him from time to time but he could read nothing in her eyes.

They came to a short valley, that spread downtrail for a mile with grass enough for a few hundred head of stock, a clutch of trees at one end and plenty of water.

'Wouldn't this make a nice little ranch layout?' Naomi said looking up at him.

Jim pulled up, crooked his right leg around the saddle horn and nodded. 'Put the ranch buildings down in the trees, and run a hundred head the first year. Plenty of graze, lots of water.'

'But you're not a rancher,' she said, finishing the thought for him. 'That's exactly what I've heard Ted say a dozen times. I'm not sure Ted knew what he really wanted to do with his life. Do you, Jim?'

He put his leg down and they moved out at a walk. 'Do with my life? I'm not a preacher. I don't want to be Governor. I'm not an explorer, and so far I don't want to invent a flying machine so we can get up there and fly like hawks. What I want to do right now...'

She laughed, breaking in over his words. When Naomi looked at him it was with a bittersweet smile that had a strange effect on Jim.

'Right now...' she said. 'I've heard Ted say that a hundred times, when we'd talk about the years ahead. Right now ... right now ... right now. Ted was a practical man, and now I'm hearing the same words, in almost the same situation.' She paused and looked at him closely. 'You two are a lot alike in a great number of ways, do you know that?'

'That's why Ted and I got along so well. But there's another way we're alike, Naomi. We both have excellent taste in picking beautiful women who are also charming, refined and gracious, like you.'

For a moment her eyes almost overflowed with tears, then she fought them back. Their mounts swung closer and her foot brushed his. For just a moment there was a longing, a wishing, a wanting that she could not hide. Jim saw her make an effort to cover it up, and then looked away.

'Jim, I don't think we should be talking this way.'

'No, of course not. I'm sorry. You're right.'

'It's been only such a very short time...'

'Absolutely. I shouldn't have said what I did.'

'I appreciate it, Jim, and I'm frankly quite flattered and moved by what you said, but...'

Her eyes danced now, her face lighted up like a schoolgirl's who had just had her first

180

surprise kiss. 'Hey, there, slowpoke, I'll race you to the bend in the stream.' And with that she was off, touching her heels to the horse's flanks, urging him into a flat out gallop.

Jim kicked Hamlet into a leisurely pace following her, moving into a gallop so he almost caught her as she passed the bend in the creek after a quarter of a mile.

She stooped and pulled her horse around waiting for him.

'You didn't try very hard,' she said, her cheeks pink from the excitement and the emotional release from the hard physical action.

'Of course I tried, Naomi. Hamlet isn't what you'd call a racehorse. He's a tough old actor who has depth and strength, but not a lot of fast. Anyway, pretty girls have been beating me at games since I was thirteen.'

She laughed at that and they walked their mounts on down the mountain. Neither of them spoke about their confidences, and at noon they stopped at a shady place beside the river and unpacked the lunch. Jim rolled out his blanket to sit on, and it was warm enough they could shed their heavy coats as they sat in the sun. Jim looked at her and saw she wore the same tight print dress and quickly glanced away.

They ate the food Chow Ling had prepared. He had even found a small bottle of wine from his supply wagon and sent it along. After the meal Naomi watched Jim until he looked at her.

She reached out and touched his arm. 'Thank you, Jim Steel. I don't think I've said that yet. Thank you for telling me what happened to Ted, and for coming all the way up here to try to find out more and to punish those who ... who hurt him. I just want to say thank you for being a nice man, at least the second nicest man I've ever known in all my life.' She looked away quickly, then stood. 'Now I think it's time that we get back on our horses and ride. Right now. Before I...'

Jim got up and took her hand. His fingers tingled when they touched hers. She turned away quickly and stepped up on her horse and rode away a few yards while he picked up the remains of the meal, rolled it up, and put it back on his saddle.

When he rode up next to her a few moments later, he smiled. 'All ready to go, Mrs. McIntosh? We should be a little over half way there.'

She nodded and they rode.

For the next hour they hardly said a word. He went first down the trail sometimes when it was a one-horse-wide path, but usually they rode side by side through small valleys that were gradually getting a little larger. They were within sight of the little village of Durango when she pulled up and turned to face him.

'I'm sorry, Jim, that I've been such a grumpy

old witch this afternoon, but I've been doing a lot of thinking, and I guess I've been reacting to the shock of an attractive man appealing to me. It isn't easy. When I married Ted I knew he was the man I'd spend the rest of my life with. Now that's all over. I'm sorry I acted so forward back there this noon. That's not really like me. I've known you for less than twenty-four hours and I practically threw myself at you. I thank you for being such a gentleman, such a good and true friend. I'll always want you as a friend, Jim. Always. Now, let's get into town so I can change clothes. Do you realize I've worn this very same dress for over three days!'

Jim laughed at her to try to lighten her big pronouncements. They moved down the trail and two hours later rode up to the Durango House Hotel, the only one in town. Jim left her at the desk and was assured by the clerk that Mrs. McIntosh got the same room she had before. Then Jim went across the street and three doors down to the assayer's office. He tossed his saddle bags on the counter.

A thin man with sunken eyes stared at Jim for a moment.

'About time we had some hard rock ore from the Devil's Gulch. That is where this ore is from, isn't it?'

'Yes, unless there's another placer-strike around here.'

'Not so you could notice.'

The man put the gold ore into two big pans

183

and took it into the back room. Jim followed and the assayer was not surprised. He had dealt with gold miners for over twenty years and knew they didn't often let their ore samples out of their sight.

An hour later both Jim and the assayer leaned against the counter.

'Now you aren't going to get all your ore that rich, but I'd say the type ore you gave me here should average out a $185 a ton. You get into a smaller vein or a larger one and it will go up or down. But that's the richest ore I've seen around here in ten years.'

Jim thanked him, paid the three dollar assay fee with silver dollars, and walked quickly back toward the hotel. The figure kept pounding over and over in his head, a hundred and eighty-five dollars a ton! He'd worked mines that made money on twenty dollars a ton ore. Jim couldn't wait to tell Naomi.

He ran across the dusty street, almost collided with a one-horse buggy, and then slowed to a walk. There were a lot of questions about Naomi that had to be answered.

But first he had to get the mine going, the tunnel, the stamping mill, the rest of the processes of turning ore into pure gold. Then he could decide what to do about Naomi. He ran up to her room and knocked.

'Who is it?'

'Jim.'

'Oh, come in.'

He opened the door and stared. She sat at a stool in front of a mirror combing her blond hair. Naomi wore a fresh yellow skirt and white blouse with long sleeves. As she turned her breasts pushed hard against the fabric and Jim caught his breath. For a moment he forgot why he had come.

'Why, thank you, Jim, that was a very nice stare,' she said. 'Now come in and close the door. What did the assayer tell you?'

He took off his hat and held it awkwardly, and all he could do was hand her the folded assayer's report.

She stood and took the report, read it quickly, then threw her arms around his neck and kissed him on the lips.

'Oh, Jim, that's wonderful! It's a real bonanza you've found. We'll all be rich!'

Jim's arms had come up when she kissed him and now he didn't want to let her go. She settled in his arms and he bent and kissed her once more lightly then released her.

'That's two mighty fine surprises in one day,' he said. Jim grinned. 'I think I liked the last surprise the best. You even smell delicious.'

She smiled and then touched her chin with her fingers. 'But now we have so much work to do. We can't get the mine producing before the snows come, but at least we can order equipment. I can stay here at the hotel and be your secretary and outside buyer. I can send letters to Denver asking about equipment and supplies.'

Jim laughed and caught her in a tight hug. 'You're the best partner I've ever had. Besides, you're the prettiest.' He promised her dinner, but first he said he had to have a bath and a change of clothes. He had left a suitcase here when he came in by stage a week ago.

\*　　\*　　\*

Later that night, after dinner in the hotel dining room, Jim brought Naomi back to her room. She motioned him inside and closed the door. 'I meant that about working on the mining things from here. I can do it, get a lot done, be a big help. Isn't that all right?'

She was not the positive partner now, she was asking him, vulnerable, unsure of herself.

He reached down and kissed her cheek.

'Naomi, I'd be pleased if you could help from here. We'll work out some lists of what we need and how we can do it, but that will have to wait a week. I'll go back to the mine tomorrow and tell Lucas the results and get things moving there again. Then I need to go to Denver. You should come to. In fact you might be more help in Denver than here. We'll talk about it on our way to Denver. You do want to go?'

'Oh, yes, Jim. Yes! And whatever you say is fine. Anything you say, Jim.'

'Good. Now I've got a long ride in the morning. You stay right here in the hotel, and

I'll be back in five or six days, then we go to Denver. Can you manage that?'

'Yes, I'll catch up on my sleep.'

'Good.' He reached down to kiss her and she was reaching up for him. They kissed tenderly, then he pushed away. 'Now, before we start a scandal, I'd better leave. I'll see you in a week.'

He watched the pleasure in her eyes as he stepped back and went out the door.

\*       \*       \*

At six the next morning Jim rode out of the livery stable and headed for the mine. He was less than a quarter of a mile from Durango when he realized a horseman was following him. Jim passed a campfire that smelled of recently wetted ashes, and a half mile farther on he knew there were two men following him. Jim kept the same pace. It looked like this was going to be a showdown so he wanted to select the time and the place.

## CHAPTER FOURTEEN

## DOUBLE TROUBLE TRAIL

Jim kept moving at the same speed so he wouldn't tip off the two men behind him. He'd find out what they wanted, but only when he had the advantage of surprise and position. He had a good spot in mind, about a mile ahead, where the trail wound through some house-sized boulders just before it slanted upward in the first real climb toward the next ridgeline.

Ten minutes later he rode into the jumble of huge stones, tied Hamlet behind one to a tree, and worked back to the front of the rock heap. He found the ideal hiding spot, a slab of rock that had fallen years ago. It was four feet high and a dozen feet long, a perfect spot for him. Jim broke off a branch of pine and tied it to his rifle barrel, half concealing it. Then he angled the Ballard over the rock and aimed it down the trail in front of him. He could see the trail from here for two hundred yards. Jim dug out four rounds for the rifle and laid them on the rock beside him, then he checked the loads in his sixgun. He had twenty more rounds in his gunbelt if he needed them.

Jim saw the riders round the bend in the trail and advance cautiously. One was dressed as a cowhand, with a high crowned wide-brimmed hat, and riding a pinto. The other man was younger, looked more like a city man, with a black suit but no tie, low-heeled boots, and a cigar in his mouth. He rode a gray.

Jim waited. He hoped that he would know them, that they were not trying to kill him, only catch up with him for some good reason. As they came Jim saw them eyeing the rocks with distrust, and keeping their hands near their guns. Jim zeroed in on the first man as his horse continued forward at a slow walk. Jim guessed now that they were not friendly. He would wait until the first one was at the twenty yard mark, then stop them.

They came closer and closer. The man in front said something to the younger one who dropped back ten yards and kept looking around. When the first rider reached the little tree Jim had picked as his twenty yard marker, Jim kept the rifle sighted on the rider's chest and bellowed so the man could hear him.

'Hold it right there, you're covered three ways. Don't move and you'll live longer.'

The man on the pinto reacted automatically, he drew his sixgun and fired twice at the rocks, the gun drawn so fast Jim knew he was a professional gunman. The rounds went wild.

Jim held his aim and squeezed the trigger. The Ballard boomed into the thin mountain air, a wisp of smoke trailed around the muzzle and Jim levered out the round and pushed in a new one as he watched the rider take the slug high in his chest. The force of the bullet pounded him backwards, tearing him off the horse and smashing him to the ground. He rolled over, tried to get to his knees, fell, and rolled on his back. A soft groan built into a scream as he tried to rise once more. He fell back and didn't move again.

Jim saw the second man whirl, send one shot at his rock, then spur his mount back down the trail. The Ballard came up and Jim sighted in carefully, raised the sights a hair, and fired. The Ballard's muzzle smoked for a second and when it cleared, Jim saw the horse going down. Its right rear leg caught the shot and broke cleanly. As the mount stumbled and fell, the rider went over its head, hit hard, rolled in the dirt and rocks but came up running and darted into heavy brush at the side of the trail. Jim could hear the man crashing brush as he continued his retreat.

Jim picked up his rounds, caught Hamlet's reins, and walked out to the dead man. There was no chance to question him. The Ballard's .56 caliber round had torn through the gunman's chest, slanted up and come out the back of his neck, taking two sections of his spinal cord with it.

Jim stared at the man for a moment. He had never seen him before. He hated killing, but sometimes it had to be done. In the war it was 'them' or 'us,' 'him' or 'me,' and the ethics of taking a life got hazy and unclear and too often quickly forgotten. Now sometimes it was the same. The man lying there at his boots would quickly have killed him if Jim had given him the chance. He proved that by shooting first.

No use to let a good horse go to waste. Jim caught the mount, tied the reins to the back of his saddle and mounted Hamlet. He rode downtrail until he came to the wounded horse making frantic sounds in its throat, furiously pawing the ground trying to stand up. Jim dismounted, approaching the wild-eyed horse from the front and soothed it, stroking its head. Then he put a .44 slug through its brain, ending its suffering.

There was no sign of the man who had been riding the gray. Without his horse he wouldn't stand a chance of keeping up with Jim, or getting ahead of him. He'd make his way back to town and have to report failure at the ambush try.

Jim worked his way back into the rocks on Hamlet, the pinto trailing behind. He tried to figure out who had attempted to kill him. Which of the men with money at Devil's Gulch would hire two men to track him down and kill him this far from the mine?

*       *       *

Jim pushed harder going back up to camp. When he arrived at the Devil's Gulch mine an hour before dark, he was surprised at the changes. The log cabin Lucas had started was complete. He had used poles for rafters and then filled it in with more straight lengths of three-and four-inch pine to make a semi-solid pole roof. A layer of wide, split cedar shakes from a red cedar tree had been nailed over the poles to form a warm, watertight roof.

Fewer miners were working at panning, Jim noticed. The water must be nearly freezing again. Jim wondered when the first snow would come.

At the tunnel he found Lucas still working a crew until it got dark. They had hauled the gold bearing ore across the bridge in a wagon and shoveled it into a twelve-foot square bin six feet high on the side of the slope above the flood line. The bin was made of logs and had one end that would come open when the ore was removed.

'Lucas, you old skinflint, you've been working!' Jim said.

Lucas waved and smacked his mule on the rump to get it moving the wagon across the bridge. The roadway had been leveled off on the far side so the wagon could back up to the very entrance to the tunnel. The vein had made a slight curve to the right as they had suspected. Jim could still see the vein of gold ore in the face and it looked larger than it had been when they started.

Outside he told the men to knock off for the day, and took Lucas aside. He unfolded the assay report and held it out to the old sourdough.

'A hundred and eighty-five!' Lucas yelped, his breath coming in an excited whistle. Tears stained his eyes as he looked up and held out his hand. 'Jim, I think you finally hit one. That whole damn mountain could be one great big gold mine.'

'Or?'

'Don't think no goldanged "or" right now, Jim. Dad blasted I figure we got to find ourselves a pint somewhere and do a mite of celebrating!'

They did, along with Johnny Johnson and Chow Ling. By the time the two pints were gone, the fire in the cabin's fireplace had burned out, so they built it up again and sobered a little as they talked and dreamed and spun their stories about other strikes in other mountains.

Jim caught himself wondering what Naomi was doing. He thought about her for a minute, reminding himself that she was just a pretty woman, and that he was not nearly ready to get married and settled down. He looked up at the blackness of the log cabin's ceiling and he could see her image.

The fire glittered in the rock and red clay fireplace. Lucas said they couldn't do any serious burning yet, not for another three days so the red clay could cure. But the fire made it warm enough inside so they had taken off their heavy jackets.

Chow Ling had brought all of his wagon load of treasures inside and now his wagon was used to haul overburden away from the mine which had formed a hard, solid road. They would need it to haul in the new machinery.

Chow had also built a swinging hook for a big iron pot so he could cook over the fire. Chow had fashioned more red clay bricks, fired

193

them himself, then used them to form a kind of stove and oven for cooking.

'Much better inside,' Chow Ling said for the twentieth time, and everyone cheered. Jim never checked when they got to sleep, but it was very late.

He found his new bed. It was a log frame nailed together and sat a foot off the floor. Strong wires had been wrapped around the logs to create a kind of flexible foundation. Then a blanket had been sewn together and stuffed with tips of pine boughs to make a yielding yet comfortable mattress. Jim sighed as he lay on it. It was the best bed he had ever had in the wilderness.

*     *     *

Jim was up at dawn, shaking his head to clear it, then had a good breakfast of oatmeal, coffee, and biscuits. His first step was at the store. Jim looked evenly at the big man behind the counter and then smiled.

'Abe, just wanted to tell you that somebody did try to wipe me out down the trail a ways.'

'Why tell me?' Lindstrom said, his voice taking on a angry note.

'Because your noising it around about my looking for Ted's killers must have done some good. I just wanted to thank you.'

'Looks like they missed,' Abe said, his eyes guarded.

194

'Several times.'

'Uh huh. How's their health?'

'One of them up and died on me before I could ask him. The other one got thrown off his horse and took off running downhill. Never had a chance to talk to him either.'

'Know them?' Abe asked.

'Never saw either one in my life.'

'Probably just as well.'

'Abe, you like to play some poker I hear. I'm trying to get up a little game this morning. You, me, and Lawton.'

Abe frowned, looked around. Nobody else was in the store. 'Might find time for a hand or two. But you and me got to have a talk. I mean about the store. You're gonna have a mine here, so I'm wondering if you're gonna have a company store too?'

'Not if you charge fair prices, and keep a good stock. You're welcome to stay. 'Course it's your land and your store. No way I can tell you to clear out. But you start gouging on prices and I'll bring in my own stock and undersell you.'

'Yeah, been done before.'

'Abe, you keep a fair profit and I won't bother you. Fact is I'll be glad to have you here and get rid of the job of having to run a company store. Now, let's go play some poker.'

Five minutes later they found Lawton finishing his breakfast and talked him into a morning game.

They settled around the table and Lawton gave Jim a new deck of cards and asked him to break and seal.

'What's your pleasure, gentlemen, dealer's choice?' Lawton asked. They nodded and Jim dealt a hand of five card stud, a dollar ante and a dollar minimum bid. The first game Jim won on a pair of jacks and a king high. It was a twenty-two dollar pot.

They played for an hour, but Jim learned little. Abe was a good poker player, taking his small profits when they came, but cutting his losses, never paying ten dollars to see a last card on a losing hand. He was not a real gambler, more a cautious and smart percentage player. He won a hundred dollars on skill and caution. Jim was twenty-five behind when Abe pulled out. He said he had to get back for the noontime 'rush' at the store. When he left, Lawton stood and stretched.

'There goes the kind of a poker player it's hard to play against. He never bluffs, he never bets when he doesn't have the cards. It's no fun. You know what he has by the way he bets. He wins and wins. If he loses he doesn't splurge. He carefully wins back his losses, then starts over again, winning another ten dollars at a time.'

'Why don't we cut for high card for fifty dollars and liven up the game a little?' Jim asked.

Lawton smiled. 'Now that's more my style of play!'

They cut. Jim turned up a nine of spades and Lawton grinned. The odds were on Jim's side, but Lawton dug into the stack and came up carefully with a card. It was a seven of clubs. Lawton swore.

'Okay, Steel, let's stop fooling around and get down to some serious poker, no limit, table stakes.'

'How much you putting on the table?'

'Two thousand to start,' Lawton said.

'Sounds about right. I've got that much in dust.'

'I need it here,' Lawton demanded.

'My word is good for it. I've never welched on a bet yet.'

They stared at each other hard for a moment, then the gambler nodded. 'I guess your claim will cover it.'

They dealt the cards. Lawton brought out two thousand dollars worth of poker chips for Jim to use and they settled down. Some pots had a hundred dollars in them. One went over two hundred. Jim began to win steadily on luck and the draw. When he was a thousand ahead, Jim noticed that suddenly his luck had turned sour. He watched Lawton and saw why. Jim watched carefully, unsheathing his knife and laying it in his lap. Suddenly his knife slammed down into the table, the point pinning Lawton's cuff and an ace of spades that was sliding out of his sleeve.

'Well, well, well. That looks like an ace up your sleeve, gambling man. How do you account for that?'

'I must have dropped the deck,' Lawton said watching him, his left hand moving toward his lap.

'Keep your hand on the table!' Jim barked. 'You may also have dropped your senses. Remember what we said about cheating?'

Jim's sixgun came out and up in one smooth motion and he was aiming the weapon at Lawton's right hand. At the same time he felt the cold steel of another gun barrel pressing against the back of his neck.

'Be very careful the next few seconds, Mr. Steel. It would be a shame if you and I got into a gunfight over a deck of cards and you got your head blown off.'

'No problem there,' Lawton said, the Derringer was now in Lawton's left hand aiming at Jim over the edge of the table. Lawton laughed. 'Give the man your gun, Steel.'

A hand reached in and Jim slid the weapon to the hand. Lawton held the small gun aimed at Jim. 'Let's say, Mr. Steel, that you have excellent eyesight and a highly developed ability to detect aberrations in this game. I'm not sure if I could cheat and get away with it, so I simply won't try. I trust you won't either?'

'I never cheat except with a cheater.' The gun

198

muzzle stayed at Jim's neck as Lawton put the Derringer away and pulled Jim's knife out of the table top.

'Then I see no reason for the weapons.' He nodded and the gun moved away from Jim's neck.

'Don't turn around, Mr. Steel. It's best that you don't know who my helper was. Now, shall we continue our friendly little game?'

They played another hour and Jim was over two thousand dollars ahead. He was sure that Lawton had not been cheating.

Jim stretched and stood. 'I hate to break a run of luck, but it's time for my dinner. We'll resume play promptly at three o'clock if you wish.'

'Your luck will change, Steel.'

'It's not luck, it's skill, Mr. Lawton.' Jim scraped his winnings into his hat, paid back Lawton $2,000 for chips and took the other two thousand in paper money and gold coins with him.

Back at the cabin, Chow Ling saw him coming and had his dinner warmed up and ready: roast rabbit with mashed potatoes, some wild onions, a kind of water cress Chow Ling had found along the Los Pinos, homemade fresh bread and butter, and coffee. Jim took an hour eating and relaxing. He even had a ten minute nap on his bed.

When he went back to the poker table he took along a thousand dollars worth of gold dust in two doeskin pouches. He talked to Lucas before he left, explaining exactly what he wanted him to do, and where he was supposed to be. Then Jim went back to the gambler's tent, a smile on his face.

Lawton was waiting, pacing the ground in front of the tent. His face was drawn, tense.

'Now, if you're ready, Mr. Lawton, you might as well continue losing money. It's harder, isn't it, when you don't cheat.'

Lawton scowled and dealt. Toward the end of the betting for the first pot Jim saw something he couldn't believe. It had been thrown in to meet a twenty dollar bet.

Carefully Jim picked up the double-eagle that had been hand crafted by an expert goldsmith. He stared at it in wonder and growing anger. There was no doubt about it. Jim had been in the Mexican village when the goldsmith had created the medallion from the twenty dollar gold piece. There could only be one like it in the world, and it had belonged to Ted McIntosh. The only way to get it away from Ted would be to kill him.

Jim fingered the medallion and stared up at Lawton, a cold fury growing on his face.

# CHAPTER FIFTEEN

## THREE ACES OVER SHOTGUNS

Jim held up the gold medallion and continued to stare at Lawton. 'Where in hell did you get this?' His voice was thin, so choked with sudden emotion that he could barely talk.

Lawton tried to pass it off. 'Oh, somebody chopped up a double-eagle, but I figure there's still enough gold there to be worth twenty-dollars.'

'Who bet it, when?' Jim said with growing anger.

'Who?' Lawton laughed, his nervousness gone now, a gleam of triumph showed in his eyes as Jim became more and more agitated. 'How can I remember every miner who throws a dollar in the pot? Somebody must have bet it and lost.'

'That medallion belonged to Ted McIntosh, and he'd never bet it. It was his lucky charm. I was with him in Mexico when he had it made. He'd never bet it!' Jim was almost shouting now.

'Looks like somebody did. Now, do you want to finish the game and play some more poker, or just talk about the old days?'

Jim sat down, stared at his cards. Lawton bet twenty dollars and Jim folded.

'New deck,' Jim said, barely able to control his voice. He knew it was no kind of a mood to be in to play good poker. Not the kind of games he needed to play. He calmed himself. He tried to push the medallion out of his mind. He knew now that Lawton showed it to him with the idea of upsetting him. Jim was sure Ted would never part with the medallion willingly. He was either unconscious or dead when they ripped it off the chain around Ted's neck. Jim chased it out of his mind and concentrated on the poker game. He would take it one card, one bet, one hand at a time. The ante was twenty dollars and there was no betting limit.

It took just four games for Jim to move where he wanted to be. He won three of the four pots and now had over five thousand dollars sitting in front of him.

Jim cleared his throat and lifted his sixgun from its holster and laid it on the table.

'Mr. Lawton, I remind you of your house rules. Only poker, no fancy sleight of hand. I don't want you even to make a move that might indicate to me that you *could* be cheating, because I'll blow your head off. I hope you will understand that.'

Lawton smiled. 'Getting nervous about the high stakes, Steel? I'm playing poker, not running a magic show. No card tricks. Just be sure you do the same.' He put his .45 caliber Derringer on the table beside his stack of coins and bills and smiled.

The next game was seven card stud with Jim dealing. He dealt two cards down to both of them, and looked at his own hole pasteboards. He had a jack and queen of diamonds. The first card up to Lawton was an ace, and Jim drew a seven of spades. Lawton bet two hundred dollars and Jim covered it. The next card came up a six of diamonds for Lawton and Jim drew a seven of diamonds. Now Jim had a pair of sevens showing and a queen and jack in the hole.

'Pair bets,' Jim said. He threw two one hundred dollar bills into the pot. Lawton counted out ten golden double-eagles and pushed them forward.

The third card to Lawton was an ace, giving him a pair of aces and a seven of spades showing. Jim drew a queen and now had two pair, queens and sevens, but only the sevens showing.

Lawton grinned at his pair of aces.

'Aces are worth three hundred dollars.'

Jim met it and dealt again. He turned up a third card, an ace for Lawton who lifted his brows in pleasure. Jim caught a six of clubs for no help.

Lawton now showed three aces on top and a seven. Jim had a pair of sevens, a six and a queen up. Lawton's cards showing had Jim beaten so far even with his hole cards. Lawton sat there smiling at his hand and enjoying his advantage, the power of his three aces.

'I bet a thousand dollars, Jim. It costs you a thousand to see your last card.'

Jim grinned right back at him. 'Only a thousand? When you've got my third seven in your hand so I can't possibly draw a fourth seven? You're all heart, Lawton. You even ruined my flush.' Jim thought it out quickly. It wasn't a smart play. It was a thousand dollar gamble to see that seventh and last card, but from somewhere Jim had an urging to go ahead, to take the risk. He had over seven hundred dollars in the pot already. Jim watched Lawton count out his bet and put it into the pot. Jim pushed the two bags of gold dust into the center of the table.

'I'll see you thousand, Lawton. The last card, down and dirty.'

Jim dealt Lawton a card, hoping it wasn't another ace. He laid a card down on his two hole cards, then put away the deck and picked up the three down cards. Jim shuffled them without looking, then peeked at one. It was his queen. He shuffled them again and looked again: jack of diamonds. Lawton watched him with irritation.

'Are you going to look at your other card or not?' the gambler said.

'I'm in no hurry.'

'I think I have you beaten on the board. Shall I make a big bet and let you squirm, or check to you?'

'Whatever you want to do, Lawton.' Jim shuffled the cards again and showed the queen. He opened the other two cards and saw a glimmer of red. When he pushed back the third card he saw it was the queen of hearts. He had a full house, queens over sevens. His expression didn't change. Jim looked up with steady eyes.

'Your bet, gambler.'

Lawton laughed and began counting out coins.

'Just name it,' Jim said quickly. 'We can count it later.'

Lawton snorted. 'It's that bad, huh, Steel?' He leaned back and then concentrated on his cards a moment. He was figuring the cards out, the ones showing, and what Jim might need to best his hand. 'Hell, I'll make it easy for you. The bet is $500. That gives you a chance and won't scare you off.'

Jim stared at his cards, started to fold them, and let Lawton reach for the pot before he held up a hand stopping him.

'Whoa, there, pardner. I'll see your five hundred and raise you a thousand.'

Lawton's hand stopped in mid air, his face a curious mixture of disbelief than of anger.

'You're bluffing me with a pair of sevens and a queen. It's got to be a bluff. You must think I'm crazy. You can't have more than three sevens because I've got one. You could have another queen, lots of combinations. But I don't believe you do. You're bluffing. All right,

205

a thousand to match yours and I'll raise you another thousand. That's twenty-five hundred dollars to you, Steel.'

'Call,' Jim said softly. 'Now, let's count out the money and get it in the pot so there aren't any misunderstandings. We each owe the pot twenty-five hundred dollars.'

It took several minutes for them to count out stacks of coins and bills, then double-check each other before they pushed all the money and bills into the pot. Much of it was in twenty-dollar gold pieces, and lots of paper bills. When it was done, Jim realized there was over six thousand dollars on the table between them.

'I called, Lawton, show me what you've got.'

Slowly Lawton put down his cards, three aces on top and a seven and a nine and a king in the hole.

Jim didn't say a word. He put up his two sevens, and his queen, then laid down his jack, then a queen paired up and after a short pause he put down the third queen.

'Full house, queens over sevens. You lose, Lawton.'

The gambler stared at the cards for a minute, then sighed.

'Yes, I've been having a run of bad luck ever since you came into camp. Looks like it's time I changed my operation. Most of the money is gone here now, anyway. And a mine you run would never have a good gambling town. You'd keep too tight a rein. So I think it's time

I was moving on.'

'Good idea,' Jim said. He reached for the money. A knife thunked into the table, the wide blade stabbing through a fifty dollar bill and sank into the table two inches from Jim's wrist.

'But I'll be taking the pot with me,' Lawton said. 'And the rest of the money you have. You see, I have the best hand after all. My hand is standing right behind you.' Lawton motioned to Jim. 'Yes, go ahead and look. It won't matter this time at all.'

Jim turned and saw Abe Lindstrom and Winslow Carter both holding sixguns aimed at him.

'Carter, I expected you, but not Abe. What happened, Abe, did you lose your store to Lawton in a poker game?'

'Not really, Steel,' Lawton said. 'Although it doesn't matter now, because you won't be telling anyone. The fact is Abe Lindstrom never did own the store. He fronted it for me. It's my store. Abe just worked for me.'

'And Carter,' Jim said. 'You needed somebody on the Miner's Committee you owned, so you picked Carter and got one of the other three shot. Carter was the best man you could find to buy.'

Carter shivered and glared at Jim. He still had a heavy bandage around his leg and walked with a limp.

'Don't say that, Steel,' Carter said. 'I have to

make a living, too. And besides, I owe you for trying to kill me with that buffalo gun.'

'Shut up, Carter,' Lawton said. 'Get his other gun, Abe.'

'Don't do it, Abe. You're in enough trouble already. Take a look outside, Abe, out the front flap.' Jim let him get to the flap, then he yelled loudly. 'Lucas, now!' There was an immediate roar of a shotgun and Abe jerked his head back in.

'God almighty!' he said. 'I thought I was hit.'

Lawton stepped to the tent flap and looked out.

'That's six shotguns you're staring at, Mr. Lawton,' Jim said. 'Looks like *I've* got the best hand after all. Those are ten gauge shotguns with enough heavy buckshot to blow this tent apart. Better have your men put down their iron, and they won't get hurt.'

'The money?'

'Mine, Lawton, I won it. You can keep what you didn't bet.'

Lawton tried to smile. 'Well, the end of a run of bad luck isn't usually so drastic. Put away the guns, boys. Give them to Steel here, he's our lawman.'

When Jim had the guns he told the three men to sit on the floor, then called to Lucas. The old miner boiled through the door tent flap like a sinner-hunting preacher and chuckled when he saw the lineup on the wooden tent floor.

''Pears like you've been doing some skunk

huntin', Jim.'

'True. Just which one smells the worst I'm not sure.' He stepped in front of Winslow Carter. The man's leg stretched out in front of him where the heavy bandage still protected the rifle shot wound.

'Carter, I should have let you bleed to death that night.'

'Why for God's sakes?'

'It's easier on a man than hanging,' Jim said.

'Hanging? I'm not hanging.'

'You participated in a bushwhacking where a man was killed, you're charged with murder.'

'Hey, no! They didn't tell me it was a kill. Honest! Lawton himself told me just to sit there and...' He stopped.

'Shut up, you fool, Carter,' Lawton snapped, furious.

'You go on taking orders from Lawton and you'll hang for sure. Now what about the two men who tried to gun me down on the trail?'

Carter scowled, glanced at Lawton, then looked up. 'Lawton sent one man out to kill you. He picked up a friend in Durango. They were to get you on your way back, after you left the woman. I heard Lawton give the orders.'

'Now you're getting smart, Carter. You may not hang after all. What about the redhead who drowned under his sluice? Did you kill him a month ago up here?'

'Who?'

'The redhead, a big man, Ted McIntosh.

209

Naomi McIntosh's former husband.'

'Oh, God, no! I didn't do that. I wasn't working for Lawton then. I didn't even know...'

Jim kicked Carter's wounded leg and the man screamed. When he could speak again he shook his fist at Jim. 'Dammit, I didn't have anything to do with that. Lawton did it himself. McIntosh won too much at poker, then caught Lawton cheating and was gonna run him out of camp. He got pistol-clubbed from behind and Lawton held him under the water by himself.'

'And you'll testify to that in miner's court?' Jim asked.

Carter remained silent.

Jim kicked his wounded leg again and Carter screamed. He began sobbing and tears worked down his cheeks. He nodded.

'I didn't hear you, Carter.'

'Yes, I'll testify,' Carter said.

Jim swung his fist and hit Lawton on the cheek, flopping him flat on the floor from his sitting position. He snarled and started to jump up, then he slumped down, fear, terror, and fury showing on his face.

'That's not evidence!' he screamed. 'You can't convict me on his word alone!' Lawton said.

Jim ignored him. 'Put your hand on the floor, Lawton,' Jim ordered. Lawton held back, then as Jim aimed his sixgun at the man's

210

head, Lawton lowered his hand to the floor.

'Your right hand, palm down, and spread your fingers.'

He did.

Jim fired the .44 once. The slug slammed between the outstretched thumb and finger. Lawton yelped in surprise and tried to jump up. Jim's boot on Lawton's shoulder held him there. The second shot went through the back of the gambler's hand, smashing a dozen delicate small bones that make up the mechanical marvel of the hand. Lawton screamed, blubbered in agony on the floor as the sound of the shot echoed away down the canyon.

'Lucas, have one of your men go get Stephano, we're going to have a trial before sundown.'

Jim had a long, private talk with Abe Lindstrom. He never had taken part in any of the killings that Lawton had engineered. Lawton's two top gunmen had left camp a week ago. One of them was the man whose arm Jim had broken across his knee.

'I was the store manager, that's all. Carter made me come today because the other troops were all gone.'

Jim told him to get back to the store. Then he stopped. 'Do you know anything about the killing of Ted McIntosh?'

Abe nodded. 'I heard three of them talking about it in the store one night. They were drinking and talking. I heard Lawton order them to help him. He said later after dark they'd take McIntosh to the creek and drown him. I'll testify.'

Jim nodded and sent him back to the store.

\*    \*    \*

They had the trial at five that afternoon. Half the miners were there. It was duly constituted and declared. Lawton screamed for twenty minutes before they put a gag on him. The trial was over in a half hour. Lucas had been named to the Miner's Committee and voted guilty with the other two.

Just at dusk, Jim stood looking at the hanging-tree. Lawton's body swung in the gentle breeze. It would be there for twenty-four hours, then buried in an unmarked grave. Jim decided he would allow no more professional gamblers in Devil's Gulch.

He started for his cabin and again he wondered what Naomi was doing.

## CHAPTER SIXTEEN

## THE BEST OF BOTH

Far into the night Jim and Lucas worked on the small table under light from a coal oil lamp.

They laid out plans for the mine and what they needed to do first. They decided early that they would not be able to get into actual production before winter, but they would do all they could until bad weather stopped them.

'We keep digging back on the vein and build a couple more log bins outside to put the gold ore in beside the other one,' Lucas said. 'Then when we get snowed in, we just stop.'

'First on our list should be housing for the men,' Jim said. 'We need to build those two dormitory log houses.' Jim paused and rubbed his chin. 'Enough room for twenty men. Two buildings about this size should do it. Bunks two high and two fireplaces in each one.'

'Really should have the dormitories on this side of the river,' Lucas said. 'Back far enough so the spring runoff won't flood them.'

'When the last of the placers quit their claims we can extend your hard-rock claim over to this side of the river and chop off some on the far end. That way we'll own the land where we put the dormitories.'

'Tarnation, even after it starts to snow and we can't move the wagons any more, we can still cut timbers,' Lucas said. 'We can keep part of the crew working all winter, and feed the rest. Hell's bells, we'll need cross-ties for the rail lines, and square-sets and bracings. We can have a whole stack of them by the time the snow melts.'

By midnight they had talked it out, made

lists for supplies for machinery, equipment, food. Jim had three long rows of items he should get right away, some needed soon, and the rest after the first thaw. They had their work projects set on a priority basis with the housing coming first.

The next morning Jim called as many of the gravel washers around him as were interested and he told them about the high yield of the ore from the assay report. He told them about the winter work and what they hoped to do. Twenty more men said they would sign on and report to work that morning. Only two were still on their placer claims now. Jim put the men to work clearing land and leveling the two spots for the barracks.

Jim watched Winslow Carter ride out of camp. Carter had agreed to leave as soon as the trial was over. Jim decided Carter wasn't one of the killers, just a weak man easily led.

Preacher Stephano decided to stay after all, so they still had their Miner's Committee.

Jim stayed two more days, made sure everything was moving along well, and then packed his saddlebags. He had brought the guard in from his lookout position. They hadn't seen anything more of the Utes, and Jim guessed that the Indians had gone south to their winter lodges where it was warmer.

The Miner's Committee had confiscated all of Lawton's goods, except the store they knew nothing about, and put the money in the

Devil's Gulch community fund. It would be the first treasury of the town, to be used for hiring a marshal, or whatever was needed.

They had almost four thousand dollars in gold dust, paper money and coins in the vault. Most of the cash they had found in the tent. It made a good start for the new little community, and Jim was determined to build a town there.

It was a bright crisp morning when Jim started for Durango. Frost was on the grass as Hamlet moved out grudgingly, reminding Jim that he was an actor, a night-time horse and getting up before noon was a great imposition on him. At last the big buckskin settled down and they moved along the trail at a steady pace.

*　　　*　　　*

It was almost dark by the time Jim rode up to the livery in Durango and made sure that Hamlet was in a stall with fresh straw and given oats and hay.

Then Jim went to the Durango House hotel and took a room. He had just dropped his saddlebags on the floor when someone knocked on his door. He opened it cautiously and suddenly a swirl of pretty white dress and ten petticoats surged through the door topped with bouncing blond hair and the eager smiling face of Naomi McIntosh.

'Jim! You're finally back!' She rushed to him

215

and put her arms around his neck kissing his tired, trail-dirty face. He kissed her in return.

'I'll get your dress all dirty,' he said.

'That's why I put it on, silly, to look nice for you, so I don't care if you get it dirty, and if you don't hug me in about a minute I'm just going to explode!'

He hugged her then and both started talking at once, then they laughed and at last they sat down on the bed.

He told her about the lists of equipment they needed and that they could start for Denver in the morning, or whenever the stage came. Then carefully, factually and as gently as possible he told her what he found out what happened to Ted and how his killer had been tried, convicted, and hanged.

Naomi cried, then dried her tears and cried again. When she was done he dried her tears, walked to the window and patted her face with a handkerchief. When Naomi came back she smiled at him.

'Jim Steel, you are the best friend any man ever had. I'm sure Ted thanks you, and I thank you, and I shall go on thanking you for just years and years. I don't know how I have been so exceptionally lucky to know two such marvelous men.'

She changed then, suddenly her eyes were snapping, her chin came up and she stood. 'Now, I'll get out of here and order up a tub full of hot water so you can have a relaxing hot bath. Then we'll have a long, luxurious supper. After that you may come to my room for some cards, or talk or we can have an official partnership session.'

Jim grinned. He had seldom seen a prettier lady, and now she was radiant, her blond hair curled just slightly, and her cheeks were pink with excitement.

'Don't you even want to see the present I brought you in my saddlebags?'

She shook her pretty head.

'Mr. Steel, I'm not that interested. I have everything I want, I am a totally happy and contented woman, and I'm getting hungry, so why don't you hurry with your bath?'

'Yes, ma'am.'

'I could stay and wash your back,' she said.

'You could, but you probably won't.'

'You're right.' She walked to the door, laughing softly at his expression. 'Now hurry. I've been waiting days for this fancy supper.'

\*     \*     \*

They had the most expensive meal the hotel could offer and a bottle of their best wine. When they reached Naomi's room after the supper, she opened the door and welcomed him inside.

'Jim, that wine has made me just a little tipsy.'

'Then we'll have no board of director's

meeting.'

She stood close to him and kissed him and Jim held her and kissed her seriously. They sat down on the bed and she leaned back then reached up for him.

'Naomi, do you think it will be all right?'

'Yes, Jim, I know it will be. I've been thinking about it for a week.'

'Nothing serious. For as long as we both want to, and it's interesting and exciting and thrilling for both of us, right?'

A frown touched her forehead. 'A woman likes something a little more permanent. I was hoping . . .'

'But you see, I'm not the marrying kind. Not yet, not nearly yet.'

'Maybe I can change your mind,' Naomi said.

'You certainly changed Ted's.'

'I did, didn't I?' She grinned. 'I can always try to change yours too.' She looked up and smiled then slowly began opening the twenty-four closely spaced buttons down the front of her white dress. Her hand stopped suddenly. 'Oh, you said you brought me a present.'

Jim eased off the bed and got something out of his saddlebags he had left there when he picked her up for supper. It was a buckskin pouch. He gave it to her.

Naomi opened the drawstring and looked in. It was filled with Devil's Gulch gold dust.

'How much?' she asked, properly impressed.

'Over a thousand dollars worth of gold.'

'That's very nice.' She leaned up and kissed him her thanks, then she settled back on the bed, pulled the drawstring on the gold dust and put it to one side.

'Jim, that was really very thoughtful of you, but now why don't we get back to the more important things?' Her hand continued unfastening the buttons on the front of her dress, and Jim bent down and kissed her.

We hope you have enjoyed this Large Print book. Other Chivers Press or G. K. Hall Large Print books are available at your library or directly from the publishers. For more information about current and forthcoming titles, please call or write, without obligation, to:

Chivers Press Limited
Windsor Bridge Road
Bath BA2 3AX
England
Tel. (01225) 335336

*OR*

G. K. Hall
P.O. Box 159
Thorndike, Maine 04986
USA
Tel. (800) 223–6121 (U.S. & Canada)
In Maine call collect: (207) 948–2962

All our Large Print titles are designed for easy reading, and all our books are made to last.